The Bathhouse

BOOKS BY FARNOOSH MOSHIRI

The Bathhouse
At the Wall of the Almighty

The Bathhouse

A Novel

FARNOOSH MOSHIRI

Beacon Press
BOSTON

Beacon Press
25 Beacon Street
Boston, Massachusetts 02108–2892
www.beacon.org

Beacon Press books are published under the auspices of
the Unitarian Universalist Association of Congregations.

First Beacon Press edition published in 2003
Printed in the United States of America

07 06 05 04 03   8 7 6 5 4 3 2 1

This book is printed on acid-free paper that meets the uncoated
paper ANSI/NISO specifications for permanence as revised in 1992.

Text design by Isaac Tobin

Library of Congress Cataloging-in-Publication Data is available.

To the memory of the prisoners of conscience who were executed in the prisons of the Islamic Republic of Iran and to M. Raha, whose memoir inspired this work of fiction

and

For David and Anoosh
who give me love and support

"When the full moon comes out, look around."

— *Rumi*

I

That hot August night, as usual, twenty minutes before the curfew, Mali left for work. At ten the lights went out. I locked the doors and sat by the window. I rested the candle on the floor so that it wouldn't attract attention from outside. The moon was swimming among the dark clouds; it was not full yet, the lower edge needed to become round. Now it looked like a chipped porcelain saucer. Just a month ago at this time all the neighbors—believers and nonbelievers—started the week-long parties on the roofs. They ate watermelon and discussed the existence or non-existence of the Sacred Face of the Great Leader on the moon. But now everybody was caged in. The party was over.

The heavy biology book open on my lap, I looked across the yard at the silhouettes of our neighbors walking about in their bedroom. This sight always made me feel secure. I was not alone; Mr. and Mrs. Dorri were on the other side of the yard. If I'd open the window and scream, they'd hear me and come to my rescue.

Since the army had recruited their only son, sending him to the Holy War, the couple hadn't had a full night's sleep. Arash was only one year older than I was, we were playmates when we were kids. His last year of high school we played less and talked more. We went to the movies a few times and once he took me to a birthday party where we danced together. I remembered that his palm touching my back was wet with sweat and I wanted the endless music to end. Now that he was a soldier, fighting in the remote parts of the country with the invisible enemy, I missed him and felt sorry for him. No one was sure if he'd ever come back. I sat behind the dark window imagining his small delicate hand shaking and sweating while holding a machine gun.

Mr. and Mrs. Dorri walked ghost-like through their house, as if looking for him. They roamed the rooms in different directions, holding candles in their hands. Most mornings, the moment Mali arrived from the hospital, they rushed to our door to inquire if the night before, by any chance, they had brought in wounded soldiers. Mali laughed, assuring them that had she seen Arash among the soldiers, she'd have called them immediately.

The green digits of my watch flashed 10:55. This was my father's last watch. After losing his old Swiss watch, his wedding present from my mother's father, he bought this inexpensive digital watch with a calendar and a chronometer all in one. He was fascinated with his cheap watch, because it had many functions and the digits were luminous green and shone in the dark. When he and Mother died in a car accident, a policeman handed us a plastic bag containing their belongings (one of my mother's broken turquoise earrings, half of my father's tie, smashed shoes, and so on). I took Papa's watch, wearing it ever since. I told myself that as long as the batteries of this watch work, Papa will be with me. When the batteries die, I'll forget him.

Now, at 10:55, Mr. Dorri left his bed, roamed through their house with a candle and returned to bed. I was waiting for Mrs. Dorri to wake up and make her round when our doorbell rang. In our two-story house (the second story had been empty since our parents' death) the ring always resonated alarmingly. My heart froze for a long moment before I could stand up. Another long ring. I knew that this wasn't my brother because he always rang in his special rhythmic way: one long, two shorts, and two longs. I pushed the button on the intercom and asked who it was.

"Open!" a voice ordered.

"But, who is it?"

"I said open!"

It was them. I had no doubt about it. They were after my brother. I didn't know where he was, so I didn't panic. I remained calm, just standing there, thinking. Ring, ring, ring. Then a longer ring. More delay and they would break through the gate or climb the walls. I glanced at the Dorris' window. Pitch dark. Both were in bed. I pressed the button, hearing the doorbell's long buzz. Now I stood in the middle of the room and listened to the footsteps on the corridor's tiled floor. Heavy boots. Several. Then the door opened and they came in.

2

One of the five guards was a young boy, maybe even younger than me; he didn't have much hair on his face except for a few long strands hanging on his chin and cheeks. He had opened his legs, leaning the butt of his machine gun against his waist and squinting one eye like an American movie star—a Clint Eastwood or something. Their commander, a bearded man, stocky and pot-bellied, ordered the kid to follow me to my room and guard the door when I got dressed. Meanwhile, the other guards ransacked the living room, Mali's room, the kitchen, and the study. They pulled most of the books off the bookshelves and threw them on the floor. Father's gold-rimmed, handwritten version of Omar Khayyam fell apart. The yellow leaves spread across the room. They dumped a few books into a huge garbage bag, including hard-covered Russian novels my mother had read all her life.

In my room, I pulled on my gray long-sleeved school uniform. I didn't have anything uglier than this. I wore a scarf, too. Although it had not become mandatory to wear veils yet, I thought it would be helpful, would keep me safe. Then I felt cramps in my belly. I reached under my skirt to see if I was bleeding, but the boy kicked the door open, jumping into my room. He prodded me with the butt of his machine gun, cursing.

"Out, out, bitch! What did you want to hide under your skirt?"

I realized that he had been watching me getting dressed. Now the other guards rushed in and ransacked my room. They took all of the four volumes of my stupid journals and dumped them into their bag. These were the accounts of my sentimental fantasies— my handsome doctor husband and our bright future, me becoming a doctor and making this house into our private clinic (in the first volumes); and in the recent volumes (under the influence of my brother and his wife) making the house into the common property of the people and only working for the clinic. I had tried to write a few poems too, describing my moods, or trees in our yard. I hadn't written about my parents' death.

A black van was parked in the street. The bearded guard slid the door open and pushed me in. On the two benches, facing each other, men and women sat, blindfolded.

"Do you know anyone here?" the pot-bellied guard asked.

I recognized my brother Hamid from the olive green shirt I had bought him for his thirtieth birthday, just a few months ago. His wife, Ferial, sat opposite him with the rest of the women. It was ridiculous to say I didn't know them.

"That's my brother," I said, "and this is my sister-in-law."

"Good girl! Now let me blindfold you!"

"But this is a mistake," I protested for the first time. "I'm not a political—"

"Close your mouth, bitch!"

"She is right, Brother," Hamid said. "She doesn't know anything." My brother was trying to be polite with the guards. I had never heard his pleading tone before.

The guard slapped him on his mouth. In the brief instant

before the total darkness of the blindfold, I noticed that my brother's face was red and swollen. This slap couldn't have caused all those bruises; they had hit him before. They sat me next to Ferial and the van took off. After a minute, I felt Ferial's hand on mine. It was ice-cold and slippery like a dead fish. A shiver ran through my spine. I wished she'd remove her hand.

"Don't worry," she whispered. "They'll let you go. Pray for me, I'm pregnant!"

3

The van stopped. They pushed and prodded us to make a line in front of an old gate. I was surprised that no one checked our blindfolds. Mine had slipped down, sitting loose on my nose. I saw an old wooden gate with two crooked lanterns on top of the wall on either side. I stood ahead of the women in the line, behind the men. My brother was in front of me. A guard pressed a button on the gate, as if this was a house. A bell rang. A minute later, a woman wearing a black chador, but leaving her whole face visible, opened the gate. I noticed that her eyebrows were trimmed and penciled all the way to her temples, forming two thin Arabian daggers above her charcoal-black eyes. There were some pock marks on her face. We moved. A guard shouted, "Put your right hand on the shoulder in front of you." I rested my hand on Hamid's shoulder and squeezed it. He whispered what Ferial had whispered earlier, "They'll let you go in a few hours. Be strong!"

The courtyard we entered was a ruined public bath. At the bottom of the round empty pool there were mud and patches of old rain water. Once, maybe in the last century, this had been a pool of fresh water for the bathers to wade in. There were chambers around the circular courtyard which, probably in old times, had served as locker rooms. As we passed in a single file toward an old wooden door, I thought I heard the faint moaning of a woman rising from one of the chambers. Before the wooden door opened and the guards prodded us into a corridor, I looked at the sky for the last time to see the moon. It was there, cold and inaccessible, floating smoothly like a weightless disc. Its surface was blank.

I was shocked to see so many people in the long hallway. People in blindfolds sat on the floor, against the wall. Some lay with their feet bandaged up to their knees. There was no air in the corridor. No fan, no open window. The strong odors of alcohol, human sweat, vomit, and urine turned my stomach. Doors on either side of the hall opened and closed constantly, people went in and out. I could hear different sounds of slapping and smacking on bare human skin. And then I heard the distinct sound of whoop . . . whoop . . . whoop. . . . From somewhere a woman screamed, "No. Stop! Don't . . . I've seen it; yes, with my own eyes—"

A female guard in a black chador covering her from head to foot, leaving only the center of her face out, approached me. She tightened my eye band angrily, squeezing my scalp as if pressing a pomegranate with all her might to get the juice out. Now I felt something around my neck and in a second I was pulled by a leash. I felt like a blind goat on the way to the altar.

When the woman pulled me down the hallway I thought that she separated me from my family because my case was different. They only wanted to ask me a few questions and then let me go. So I planned ahead: I'll go home and call Mali, tell her everything; we'll talk to our uncle who has lawyer friends. Maybe we can do something for Hamid and Ferial. A large sum of money. Our inheritance money . . . to bribe the guards. We'll get them out.

Now I felt that I was in one of those rooms off the long hall-way. I heard the legs of metal chairs scratching the bare cement floor. The woman ordered me to sit on a chair. Later I realized that the chair was facing a wall. Now she said, "I'll go and get you the forms. If you write the truth, you'll go home before morning." She left me in the dark.

I thought that of course I would write the truth, why shouldn't I? The truth was that I was not a member or even a fol-lower of any organization. I'd just graduated from high school and was studying for medical school. I was neither a nationalist nor a Marxist nor a follower of any other ideology. I was just a little selfish girl who was immersed in her own life while most youth were struggling for freedom and justice. No, I wouldn't say the last part. What did I know about my brother and his wife? Nothing. I didn't even know the full name of their organization. And their team house of course was underground—no one except them-selves and their teammates knew where it was. That was it. That was the truth and all that I knew.

Now I felt someone weeping in the room. I was not alone.

"Who is here?" I said softly.

"Hush! Shut up!" the weeping woman said.

"Did they beat you?"

"Shut up, I said."

She didn't trust me. I shouldn't trust anyone either. Maybe the guards disguised themselves as inmates to get information.

For a long time, I sat motionless in the dark, facing the wall. Once I stretched my arms, touching the cold wall with the tips of my fingers. I was tempted to remove the blindfold. I would if it were not tied so tightly. I raised my head trying to look around from under the cloth. I couldn't.

Finally the door opened and someone came in. Whoop … I felt a sudden blow on my head. The shock was more disturbing than the pain itself. Someone had struck me with something like a rubber ruler. It wasn't a baton, the kind that policemen hung from their waists; it felt flat and narrow like a ruler, but elastic, rubbery.

"Remove your eye band and fill out the forms."

This was a man's voice. I felt terrible cramps in my belly again and the sensation of something hot running down between my thighs. Was it blood? What if my skirt should get wet with blood? I felt more cramps—unmistakably menstrual cramps. Every month I had five full days of heavy bleeding. Damn, I whispered. Whoop … Another blow. My scalp was on fire.

The man shouted, "Did you hear what I said? Remove the eye band and fill out the forms."

My hands were shaking. The female guard had tied two tiny knots behind my head; I couldn't untie them. The man became impatient and pulled the eye band, removing my scarf and plucking a bunch of my hair out with it. I screamed. He slapped me.

"No screaming here! No bitching! Hear me? Now fill out the forms, you dirty little leftist."

"But I'm not—"

"Shut your mouth and write!"

I raised my head and saw his profile. He was a square man with big belly—either the same man who invaded our house or his brother. There was a huge yellow circle in the armpit of his pale blue, wash-and-wear-shirt. It was wet with sweat, sticking to his greasy skin. I didn't see his face. Now he was behind me.

Biting my lips and trying to bear the cramps, I looked at the forms. Sweat bubbled inside my hair, dripped down my forehead, and crawled on my nose. Not even a fan? Was this a torture? Each typed question had a blank space under it, as in school tests. It started with name and address and names of family members and their ages and so on. I filled it in without delay. I wanted to go home before Mali arrived at eight o'clock. On the second page the questions were political. Name your organization, name your leader or leaders, your responsibility, and so on. I left them blank. I was almost through with the first form when the man approached me, peeked over my shoulder and whipped me with that silly ruler again. This time he whipped my face. My right cheek burned and then began to pulsate.

"What is this crap, huh? Who are you fooling?"

"It's all true, sir. I've never been a member of any—"

"Are you fooling me? You and your family are all godless leftists. I'm going to bring your sister here, too. And I know what kind of trash your parents were... "

"My parents are dead... " I burst into tears.

"Shut up now! You see? You're bitching again. Fill out the second form."

Now he approached the other woman whom I couldn't see. She was weeping unceasingly, mumbling something between her hiccups.

"Brother Jamali, my baby is hungry. Please let me feed her."

"She'll be fine. She is with the sisters. Revise your second page, then you can feed your baby. You can even take her to the cell with you."

"But I've written the truth. Why do you pressure me to lie?"

"You arrogant bitch!" I heard the whoop sound of the rubber ruler.

Brother Jamali left the room. I kept staring at the second form. It was hard to believe. They were asking detailed religious questions, things that only students of theology might have known. I hadn't even learned how to pray. The words of prayers were not in my language. Praying and fasting weren't practiced in my family, nor were they taught in the schools I went to.

"Mali," I whispered my sister's name and my eyes filled with tears. "You'll go home in few hours and I won't be there."

4

We were locked up together, the weeping woman and I. The room was at the very end of the long corridor, a small dirty room with spider webs hanging from the ceiling and balls of dust on the floor. The cement floor smelled of urine, as if people had peed here many times. One small square window was on top of the wall. If there was a stool, one could climb it and look outside. A smaller window was close to the floor. The glass was painted chalk white and I could see the shadows of the iron bars on the outer side.

They had given us black chadors, but Instead of wearing them, we spread them on the floor and sat facing each other, deaf and mute. Since my cell mate earlier had told me to shut up, I didn't attempt to communicate with her. She was thinking about her baby. I could understand. But could I? For the first time I remembered what Ferial had told me in the van. She was pregnant. Thinking about her opened a hot flood inside my belly. I bled again. My underwear and my skirt were wet with blood. Blood dripped down my thighs. I couldn't talk about this with Brother Jamali. I had to wait for a female guard.

Now I heard a key in the keyhole. The door opened and Jamali came in with a little boy. The boy was not more than six. He was carrying a pitcher of water and some paper cups.

"This is Ali, my son," Jamali said. "He is the water-carrier tonight. Baba, our janitor, is sick. Give each of them a cup of water,

Ali, but don't touch them, they're not clean!"

"I need to talk to a woman."

"The sisters are short of staff. Wait till morning."

I looked at my watch. It was already four-thirty in the morning. I took the water from Ali and smiled at him. He didn't smile back. His face was puffed up, pale and stony. Jamali and his son left; Jamali banged the door and locked it after them. I lay down on the large black chador. My back felt good. Another gush of blood flooded out. I let it pump out of me, flowing under my body. From where I lay I could see the sky through the window. It was not dark anymore. The dawn was spreading its transparent net. I felt a strong urge to open the window and inhale the cool, moist air, an urge to drink the dew. That small cup of lukewarm water had made me thirstier. I imagined sipping the dewdrops like a bee drinking from a rose petal. Then I heard my cell mate weeping, the sound muffled by her palms. She mumbled something between her sobs.

At dawn a tall metal mountain collapsed. It was huge and near. It shook the walls. I opened my eyes and immediately looked at the green digits of my watch. Five. I had slept only half an hour. I could barely move my stiff body. Blood had dried on my skin and on the black chador. I looked at the woman. She was sitting up, leaning against the wall, holding a baby in her arms. The baby was quiet, sucking the woman's breast, with munching sounds. In the milky light of early morning the woman's face was pale as yellow marble, smooth and serene. She was a different person. Tranquil. Absent. She didn't even notice me gazing at her. She was looking up at the window. Her eyes were large and honey-colored, with some green specks around the irises. The black scarf had slipped onto her shoulders and her smooth light brown hair spread around her neck. The baby's head was bald. She had a patch of thin blond hair in the middle of her scalp. Now I heard munching and moaning sounds, even gulping. The woman saw me finally. I smiled. She smiled back. We didn't talk.

5

At seven, Ali brought a tray with two paper cups of tea and two pieces of stale bread. He gave me a small package. I opened the brown paper bag and found a square piece of cotton. Brother Jamali had sent me this. What could I do with it? I needed tons of sanitary napkins, not a small piece of cotton. I took it anyway. I didn't smile at Ali. He was not a child. I couldn't tell what he was.

The tea had a chemical taste. I ate the stale bread and washed my burning eyes with the cold tea. I soaked the cotton in the cup and massaged my eyes. My mother used to do this. At seven-thirty they took us out to stand in the toilet line. There were two parallel single files: men's and women's. The lines were long. I couldn't see the end of them. It would take at least one hour to get to the restrooms. But it was better than staying in the cell. We could stretch our bodies and watch the people. I searched for Hamid and Ferial but didn't see them. I saw many girls my age and even younger. I saw a few girls from our high school. They were not close friends, just acquaintances. We waved.

Some girls and boys were seriously exercising. Hopping up and down, running in place. People talked in whispers, but the minute a guard approached, they became quiet. All the guards had these funny rubber rulers and they beat us for no reason. Some men and women had black hoods on. When I looked carefully I realized that the hoods were black stockings they wore on their heads.

I was still bleeding. But I had wrapped the black chador tightly around my body so that no one could notice.

Now my cell mate, the woman with baby, talked for the first time. The baby was sleeping, laying her red face on her mother's shoulder. The woman whispered, "Did you hear that huge sound earlier?"

"Yes, it was like a mountain of iron collapsing. It woke me up."

"The wall is behind the building."

"Which wall?"

"The Wall of the Almighty."

I didn't know what to say. I'd sound naive. I hadn't heard about this wall before. So I just nodded as if I understood.

Then the woman said that her name was Zohre. She wasn't a member of any political party, but she was sympathetic toward her husband's party. She didn't tell me what party it was. Then she said that she hadn't seen her husband since yesterday morning when they arrested them. She was worried about him. What if he was one of the eighty they executed this morning?

"Eighty?" I almost screamed.

"Yes. That huge sound."

Hot blood gushed out of me again. I grabbed my belly and bent, almost kneeling on the floor. Then I felt the whoop of a rubber ruler on my neck.

"Don't sit, devil, this is not your living room. Get up!"

"I need to see a Sister," I pleaded.

"What's wrong?" the bearded guard asked.

Now all the inmates and a few guards stared at me. What

could I say? I was always too shy about these matters. I couldn't even talk with my sister.

"What's wrong, huh? Diarrhea?"

The guards laughed.

"Come with me. I don't want you devils to make a mess here. Let me take you to the Sisters' room. Grab the end of the ruler."

He didn't want to touch me. I held the end of the ruler and he pulled me behind. We had to open our way through the crowded hallway. The two endless toilet lines were stretched along the corridor, not moving at all, and prisoners, interrogators, and guards constantly went in and out of the rooms, bumping into us. I was trying to focus on the men who resembled my brother. What if he'd been one of the eighty?

Now there was a red trail behind me. Blood dripped on the floor as I walked.

We reached the end of the corridor where last night we had entered from a wooden door. The guard knocked on the last door on the left and the woman with dagger-shaped eyebrows opened the door. I saw a dozen women, all wearing black, sitting on the floor around the room. A community of ravens.

"This little devil is sick. See what she wants."

The bearded guard left me there. The woman grabbed my chador, pulled me in and closed the door.

"What is it?" Her voice was hoarse for a woman. Her nose and cheeks were full of measles marks, but her eyes were piercing. The whites were red-veined, the irises were charcoal black. I stared at her—at her strange eyes and long eyebrows. Why had the authorities let this woman pencil her eyebrows?

"What's wrong, huh?"

"I'm bleeding."

"I thought I sent someone a piece of cotton earlier. Wasn't it for you?"

"It wasn't enough. I'm bleeding a lot. Look!" I pulled the chador up just enough for her to see my calves. Blood dripped on the floor.

"Yach! This devil is dirtying here, Sisters. Give her a mop to clean the floor."

The other women who were drinking tea (was it the same smelly tea they'd given us earlier?) all stared at me. One of them gave me a piece of wet burlap and ordered me to squat and clean the blood.

"But first I need to use the restroom. I need dry underwear, thick pads—"

"Do you think you're in a resort hotel or something? Clean your mess first," the pock-marked woman said.

I knelt on the floor, wiping the blood, but more gushed out. I panicked. All my insides were pumping out. As I was wiping the floor, my eyes blurred and I thought that I was Ferial and I was losing my baby. My baby was slipping out of me on the floor of the female guards' room and I couldn't prevent it. This was not just a fetus, this was a baby the size of Zohre's baby, but slimy and slippery and it was sliding out of me with an endless stream of blood. Then I thought I'd rather lie down here and get some sleep close to my bloody child.

6

The green digits of my wristwatch showed 12:05. I was lying on the floor of our cell, under the window, where I'd slept earlier. I looked around to find Zohre and her baby. But they were not here. Instead, an older woman was sitting, knees folded into her chest. I couldn't tell her age. Fifty? Sixty? Her face was puffed up and her eyes were red. She rocked herself like a pendulum. That's all she did—hugged her legs and rocked. Another woman slept by the door. A pile of black chador covered her. I couldn't see her face.

"Hello," I said.

"Good day, my dear," the older woman said in a warm voice. "You slept so deeply that I envied you. I haven't slept for forty-eight hours."

"When did they bring me?" I asked.

"You were sleeping right here when I came."

I sat. I was dry. I had a thick pad (maybe two or three) between my legs. But I wasn't washed. Blood had dried on my legs. My belly hurt a little and felt very small, as if touching my back. I felt that I had lost a lot of weight, a heavy burden. Then I remembered the Sisters' room and the way I'd passed out.

"Did you see a woman with a baby here?" I asked the lady.

"No, dear. It was just you. Then they brought this poor thing. She fell asleep immediately. I envy her, too."

"Sleep, Mother." I don't know why I called her Mother.

"I can't. The minute I close my eyes I see his face."

"Whose?"

"My son's. They brought me here because of him. They want me to give information about him. About my own son!"

"Where's your son?"

"Must be here, in one of these rooms. They're whipping him. Or maybe they've sent him to the permanents' hall."

"Permanents?"

"This hallway is a temporary place. For early interrogations. They'll send us to the permanent building. Down there." She pointed to the left wall.

"You shouldn't be here." I whispered more to myself, fighting with tears.

"Why should you, my dear?" She kept calling me my dear. This softened me. I sobbed.

The woman who was buried under the pile of black chador slept in the heat all through the afternoon. Maybe they had injected her with something. The heat increased around two o'clock. Air did not circulate. We didn't have anything to fan ourselves with. We were thirsty. A while ago Mrs. Moradi and I had stopped talking because we had no energy. She had talked about her four sons. Her husband had left them many years ago, abandoned them. She talked about the youngest son the most, the one who was probably somewhere not far from us in the same hallway. His name was Hamid, too, like my brother, but he was only twenty-one. Then she talked about Hamid's manners, habits, hobbies, and even the objects in his room. She mentioned a calendar with colored pictures of athletes hanging above Hamid's bed. I told her briefly that my parents were dead. I talked a little about my sister, Mali, who was my guardian, but I didn't talk much about Hamid and Ferial. I wanted Mrs. Moradi to talk to me. Her voice was deep and didn't have a sharp edge. The slow way in which she uttered the words and stretched the syllables was soothing to my ears. She sounded like a woman who had been tired for a long time, and now this fatigue had slipped into her voice, had become part of her personality.

Now her eyes were closed, but she was still rocking herself. She moaned in a muffled way in her throat. I sat there watching Mrs. Moradi, remembering my mother. She must have been my mother's age. But Mother looked so much younger. How different Mother was. She used all kinds of lotions. She wore fine clothes and perfumes. This woman had never used cream under her eyes. No perfume ever. I imagined Mrs. Moradi sitting cross-legged on the floor in front of her old sewing machine, making an ugly dress for herself, most probably out of some old scraps of material, a former dress or an old curtain. My mother shopped from boutiques.

What would Mother do here? Could she even sit on this floor among the spider webs? Could she tolerate Brother Jamali for one minute? But how beautiful Mommy was, how refined. I remembered her books, her many books. She read several at the same time and spread them around the living room couch. She left her delicate, gold-rimmed reading glasses with thin golden or silver chains hanging off them, on the open books. She had several of these reading glasses so that she could still read even if she misplaced a pair. Her scented flowers were everywhere in the house, sitting in exotic hand-painted vases. Long-stemmed gladiolas, black roses. . . . I kept thinking about Mommy and looking at Mrs. Moradi.

Would my mother give information about Hamid?

Mrs. Moradi moaned and I decided that my mother would die here—the first day. Then I felt relieved that she was already dead.

"Hey, both of you come with me." The same female guard who took me to the interrogation yesterday called us out. I noticed that her face was hairy. There was a distinct mustache and some hair on her cheeks and chin. She just needed men's clothes to become a man. Maybe she was a man in disguise. Anything was possible here. Now this hairy guard leashed us, pulling us behind her through the hallways. I couldn't walk fast. The pads between my legs were about to slip out. Then they'd fall on the floor and everybody would see them. I walked without opening my legs, my thighs pressing the thick pads. The chador kept slipping off my head, too. I had a hard time holding it under my chin. I'd never worn this horrible robe in my life. Not only my mother, even my grandmother had never worn a chador. Mrs. Moradi didn't seem to have any problem handling her chador and walking fast. She was used to it.

The hallway was less crowded than yesterday. I remembered that there were eighty people less. I looked around to find Ferial or Hamid, I looked for Zohre and her baby, too. The inmates' faces were tired, sleep-deprived. Some had black and blue bruises, some had bandages around their heads. Bandages around feet were usual sights. Many were moving on their butts, sliding from one room to another. I saw more black-hooded people strolling in the hall, stopping sometimes to stare at a face.

For one full hour I sat motionless while Jamali interrogated Mrs. Moradi. He had her forms in his hands, reading the answers, forcing her to elaborate on or revise them.

"What do you mean by 'I've never seen his friends'? Are you kidding me, or what? I'm sure you've fed these bastards and even given them a room to sleep in."

"Never."

Whoop! I heard the rubber ruler. He hit Mrs. Moradi. I hunched, bent into myself, pulled the chador over my whole body like a tent and stuck my forefingers in my ears. I couldn't hear more of this. I couldn't hear the whoops. Now I tried to remember a long poem I had memorized for the final literature exam last year. It was a boring animal fable—"The Story of the Three Fishes". I started the tape in my head and the whole poem played for me. I didn't hear anything in the room except a muffled hubbub.

> *This, O obstinate man, is the story of the lake*
> *in which there were three great fishes.*
> *You will have read it in Kalila, but that is only*
> *the husk of the story, while this is the*
> *spiritual kernel.*
> *Some fisherman passed by the lake and saw*
> *the concealed prey...*

7

Brother Jamali turned my chair toward his own and ordered me
to sit straight. Mrs. Moradi was not here anymore.

"Why did you leave the second form blank?"

"Because I didn't have the answers."

"You didn't have them, huh?"

"No."

"Are you a Christian, or a Jew?"

"None."

"Do you have any religion?"

"I believe in God."

"You don't believe in God. You and your family are atheists.
Your father taught atheist philosophy before the revolution."

"I don't know the meaning of this word, sir."

"It means devil-worshiping. Because if someone doesn't
believe in the Almighty and his Faith, he believes in Satan."

"I don't believe in Satan," I said.

"Oh, you don't?"

"No."

"What are the main rules of the Faith? Count them."

"I haven't learnt them."

"So you're fooling me, huh? You little bastard. Stretch your
arms."

I stretched my arms forward.

Whoop! Whoop! Whoop! Whoop! He whipped my palms. I

closed my eyes and bit my lips, trying not to move. One million wasps stung my palms and pierced their sharp needles into my flesh. This was like the game I used to play with Hamid when we were younger. In that game I had to be quick enough to withdraw my hands before he slapped them. The game was called "Bring the bread and take the Kebob." If you couldn't pull your hands back fast enough, the burning slaps made them into hot kebob. Now if I'd pull my hands, Brother Jamali would get mad and hit my face. I'd seen purple faces in the hallway. I didn't want that.

"Before long, you'll learn your lesson. And I'll keep you here long enough so that you'll be able to recite the Holy Book from A to Z. You get me? You'll go to school here. You'll learn about your religion. Now get out of my sight! " He squeezed his face at me, showing his disgust. "Take this little brat out of here and bring the big ones." He yelled this into the hall, calling the hairy woman. "I don't want to waste my time punishing a little spoiled devil for not studying her lessons. I'll see her when I'm through with the big ones."

In the cell, the sleeping woman had vanished and instead Zohre was sitting, without her baby. She was weeping into her palms again. Mrs. Moradi's eyes were full of tears, but she did not allow herself to sob. Her face was swollen, all red, dark purple, and blue. My palms looked like balloons, or two red rubber gloves with air blown in them. I sat next to Zohre, curling my arm around her shoulders. Feeling my hug, she sobbed louder. None of us talked.

Around six, as my digital watch showed, they brought another woman in. She had a white hospital gown on and held the chador they'd given her like a coat on her arm. She didn't even have a scarf on. Her shiny black hair framed her delicate face. She smiled at everybody and sat next to Mrs. Moradi. She looked at her face and said, "So it's true that the bastards beat the ladies here. They just arrested me, though I was needed at the hospital. We had many wounded soldiers from the front today."

Then she talked for a while. None of us joined the conversation. Her name was Leila. She hadn't been to interrogation yet. She wasn't starving, as we were. She was full of energy.

"No more moon watching out there," she said. "Since the blackouts, if someone stays out or goes to the roof of his house, they shoot him. People are forgetting the moon and the sacred picture altogether. At least the curfew stopped this hysteria. Why is it so damn hot here? Can't we open that window? Will someone move here under the window? I want to get up there and see if I can open it. We'll suffocate here."

I moved under the window and got on all fours. My palms were painful, but I bore Leila's weight and let her use me as a stool. She stood on my back and looked at the window.

"The damn thing won't open unless we break it. But my hand doesn't go through the bars. Oh, what a sight! They're flogging someone. It looks like an empty pool and this man is lying on the dirt; someone is whipping him—on his feet. I guess they've shoved something into his mouth."

"They do the whippings in the empty pool," Mrs. Moradi said. "Do you see the chambers around the pool?"

"Yes ... one, two, three ... seven chambers," Leila said. "There is a brick wall at the end of the yard. Blood stained."

"The Wall of the Almighty," Mrs. Moradi said in a cold tone. "They haven't washed last night's blood away yet. Hadn't you heard about the Bathhouse when you were out?"

"No. Nothing," Leila said, and stepped down. "I was too busy in the hospital. Besides, I'm not involved in politics. I'm just a doctor."

"So why did they arrest you, dear? Are any relatives active?"

"No. It's my tongue that's active! I talk too much. I talk to my colleagues and patients. I guess I'm here because I couldn't hold my tongue."

"You talked against the government, I guess," Mrs Moradi said.

"No, I just said something about the picture on the moon. Because it's ridiculous. It's medieval. The shadow on the moon is the Sea of Tranquility. It's a real sea. Astronauts have seen it. People have walked on the moon, for God's sake, and the world knows this. I said this to some of my patients. One of them must have reported me."

"The moon business is not this republic's only problem, my dear," Mrs Moradi said and sighed.

"It's not a problem at all, it's lunacy." Leila sat next to me. "Our country is run by a bunch of lunatics. And I'm saying this as a person who isn't involved in politics at all."

We all laughed except Zohre who kept weeping.

Around seven the door opened and Ali came in with a tray. Food. There was one dish of rice mixed with lentils. We had to use our hands and eat out of the same dish. There were a few pieces of bread too. Not enough for everybody. Leila, assuming that Ali was a real child, held his hand and pulled him.

"Hey, you, what're you doing here, huh? Don't you have something better to do? What grade are you in? Let me guess ... first, going to second?"

Ali pulled his hand out of Leila's and rubbed it with his other hand, as if cleaning it. He frowned and ran out of the cell. He forgot his tray.

"Strange," Leila said. "He cleaned his hand."

"We're untouchables," Mrs. Moradi said.

We ate from the common dish as Leila talked to us. She was the most eloquent woman I'd ever heard. She kept criticizing the government and insisting that she was not a political person. We were all under her spell. She was a natural leader. We used a small piece of bread as a spoon and ate slowly, trying not to eat each other's share. Zohre didn't join us. We left her ration in front of her, but she didn't touch it.

8

When I opened my eyes the sky was dark. I saw the last streaks of lavender light inside the dark indigo. I turned to look at my cell mates, but the cell was empty. I sat upright, startled. What had happened? How long had I been sleeping? How come I hadn't heard the guards taking the women out? The green digits flashed 10:11 on my wrist. I must have slept less than two hours. But where had they taken my cell mates and why hadn't they woken me up? I sat in the dark and shortly the moon lit the cell. I looked up and saw it. The small square window had framed it. It wasn't full, but one night before the full. I looked at its smooth luminous surface and its dark shadows—the Sea of Tranquility.

At 10:35 the door opened and the hairy female guard came in. She had a bundle in her arms. She put it on the floor. Zohre's baby. I told her that her mother was not here. She said it didn't matter. I asked her where everybody was. She said in the toilet line. I needed to use the toilet too. But she said I was going to miss it tonight, because I was asleep; I had to wait till morning. Then she slammed the door. I sat for a minute trying to figure the whole thing out. Was this a form of torture? Not letting me using the bathroom? I stood up, walked up and down, tried not to think about my bladder or bowels. I walked from wall to wall. Only eight steps. I became dizzy.

The baby was wrapped in a thick blanket and it was hot.

Maybe I had to remove her covers? But what if she woke up? I did-
n't touch her, but looked at her face. It was pink. She was somewhere between three and five months old and, in spite of being in
prison had chubby cheeks. I thought that soon she would lose
them. Now she squeezed her face as if in pain and gave out a
shriek. She awoke, opened her eyes and screamed again. Catlike.
I'd seen babies before, relatives' babies, but I had never held one.
I unwrapped the blanket, picked her up, and tried to rock her. She
was incredibly light, almost weightless. She kept crying. I hoped
that they'd hear her in the hall and come to my rescue. What was
I supposed to do with her? I walked the length of the room—eight
steps—back and forth one hundred times and rocked her, mumbling meaningless words into her ears. I assured her that her
mommy was coming soon. But was she?

"Hush, hush, hush, hush, shoo, shoo, shoo, shoo . . . Mommy
is coming to give us some milk . . . " She kept wailing.

Finally I became tired. I sat cross-legged and lay her on her
stomach on my lap. I wasn't sure where I had learned this. Maybe
from a TV program. I thought she must have stomachache. But
she kept crying. Finally I held her in my arms; her little red face
was under my left breast, her mouth moving like a hungry fish in
an empty bowl. She was trying to suck on something, but all there
was was air. Slowly, I unbuttoned my uniform and took my breast
out. I didn't need to put my nipple in her mouth, her mouth found
it. She began to suck. She sucked and I closed my eyes, feeling a
sharp pain in my hard breast. She was not crying now, just sucking my empty breast. "God, O God, let them come now. All of
them, any of them, let them come and save this baby and me. It

hurts. Her gums are sharp like teeth, she is biting me. She is starving. God, help her. Help!"

Apparently, my nipple worked as a pacifier and she slept. I didn't move for a long time. I let her sleep deeply. Then, still holding her in my arms, I stood up and walked a little. I needed to use the bathroom. I couldn't make myself to use a corner of this room. Any minute they would bring my cell mates back. I made a desperate attempt and pushed the door's metal handle. It opened. I remembered that I heard the guard slamming the door, but didn't hear the key turning. Was this intentional? Did they want me to go out so that they could punish me for that? I would take the punishment if I could only use the bathroom. So I left the room with the baby sleeping in my arms.

9

When I entered the hallway, for a second I thought that the whole thing—from the beginning to the present—had been a dream. From last night's arrest up to the moment that I was standing with someone else's baby in my arms looking at a long, empty corridor.

There was no toilet line in the corridor, no bandaged men and women, no people moving on their butts, going in and out of the rooms, no guards with rubber rulers hitting prisoners randomly on their heads and faces, no women ravens, bearded interrogators, and hooded creatures. I was alone with this sleeping baby whose name I didn't know. I walked toward the other end of the hall where I remembered the guard took me to the Sisters' room this morning. Toilets were there.

Some of the office doors were open. They were all empty and the lights were out. But the hall was dimly lit with several yellowish bulbs hanging from the ceiling. The Sisters' room was open too, and it was pitch dark. No one was there.

I stood at the end of the corridor, not knowing what to do with the baby. The toilets were in a small area opposite the Sisters' room. But I couldn't pee while holding the child in my arms. I decided to leave her in the room and pick her up after I was finished. I held her with my left arm and, with my right, groped in the dark. I found a desk at the corner and lay the baby on it. Although I wasn't quite sure if she was old enough to roll over, I placed her far from the edge, next to the wall. Then I went to the restroom. The odor upset my stomach. The floor of the narrow restroom was flooded with dirty water. I held my breath all through and came out with my white tennis shoes wet up to my socks. I went back to the Sister's room and picked up the baby. She was calm and motionless. I panicked, pressed my ear to her heart, and listened. I heard the distinct sound of poom ... tack ... poom ... tack.... I lifted her up again. Lingering in the hallway, not knowing what to do next, I found myself standing in front of the old wooden door, the same doorway through which they brought us in last night. What if I opened it and stepped out into that strange courtyard? What if I opened the gate in the courtyard and stepped into the street? What if I walked all the way home, taking this baby with me?

Cautiously, I pushed the old door. It opened. I stood there facing the courtyard. Everybody was there. The guards, the interrogators, and the hooded people were on the other side of the pool where the brick wall was. They were on their knees, praying. A short, chubby, turbaned man was kneeling before them, farther apart. He recited the prayers and the staff repeated them. The prisoners sat on the cement floor on the opposite side of the authorities; their backs were to me. Men on the right, women on the left, they were squeezed against each other, sitting motionless, watching the believers.

I looked at the sky. A thick black cloud had covered the moon. I could see one slice of the disc sliding out of the cloud, the tip of a fingernail. Now the whole disc came out. The staff rose and raised their arms up. It was as if the whole scene was directed and rehearsed for this very moment when the moon slipped out, lighting the courtyard with its unusual phosphorescent glow.

"Allah is great!" the staff called many times.

Now a young guard, one of the devotees, with a hoarse voice shouted: "The Party is one, the Party of Allah. . ." They chanted this slogan many times and then began to beat their chests with their hands. In the dim light I saw that some men bared their chests, slapping their skin.

I was afraid that the baby would wake up. But I couldn't move; I was paralyzed. The prisoners seemed frozen too, holding their breaths like the audience of a strange play.

Now the staff sat but the turbaned man remained on his feet. He addressed the prisoners: "This is your last chance to repent and join the ranks of the believers. This way the gates of heaven will open to you. Now you're hanging over a pit of fire, any minute we can cut the rope and drop you into the burning flames. The rope of Allah is in our hands now. Our Leader is chosen by Allah and our government is the government of Allah. Come to the other side of the pool and sit in the ranks of the devotees. Your brothers and sisters will forgive you and take you in." He sat on a chair, the only chair in the courtyard.

A man came forward, yelling, "Bring them here. Let these devils learn their lesson tonight." In the dim light, I recognized Brother Jamali.

Two guards from either side of the stage (the place looked like a ruined amphitheater) brought two prisoners. The male guard dragged a man by a leash and the female guard (the same hairy woman) dragged a woman. I didn't know the man, but the female prisoner was Leila, the doctor. She still had her white gown on, but it was bloody and soiled. Her hair was uncovered.

"This woman refuses to cover herself. Let her learn her lesson tonight. And this man has insulted our Holy Leader. Give each of them one hundred lashes."

I stood there, in disbelief, with the baby in my arms—a baby who was probably starving to death. I watched the guard pushing and prodding Leila, forcing her to her knees. I turned to leave, but suddenly a woman, one of the prisoners shrieked, "There, there, on the moon. I can see Him! I can see Him with my own eyes—" Everyone rose and looked at the sky. They forgot about flogging. The female guards and hooded staff became hysterical; they screamed too, "Yes, yes, we can see Him, too. . . " Half the crowd dropped on the ground, half stared at the lustrous moon. Everything was getting out of control. Someone shot a bullet in the air and everybody froze.

"Who observed the holy face?" Brother Jamali asked.

The female inmates opened an avenue for a woman. She circled the pool and stood in front of Brother Jamali. She was holding her black chador tightly around her face, leaving only her eyes visible.

"Are you repenting, then?" Jamali asked.

"I do. Take me among yourselves and bless me," the woman said.

"Are you ready to appear on a TV program, condemning your former satanic ideas?"

"I am."

The devotees, male and female, raised their voices in unison, "One party, Party of God, one Leader, chosen by God." Now in

a faster rhythmic chant, they yelled, "Welcome home, Sister, welcome home, Sister—" One of the hooded female staff handed her
a black stocking to wear over her head.

"From this moment on you are a repentant. Wear your hood
and serve the Holy Republic," Brother Jamali announced.

Unveiling her face for a second to wear the black hood, the
woman turned toward the audience. Under the quivering glare of
the moonlight I recognized Ferial, my brother's wife.

I thought this incident would cancel the flogging, but Brother
Jamali didn't forget. They forced Leila and the young man onto
the ground again. I didn't stay to witness more. But I didn't go
inside the building, either. I kept thinking that this baby was starving and I had to do something about it. So, like an animal, I sniffed
to find food. From behind the rows of the sitting inmates, I moved
toward the right side of the building where I could smell grease. If
I could find the kitchen, I could find milk too.

10

I walked along the right wall, feeling the circular shape of the building. Then I saw a small clay hut on the left, lit only by a dying candle. Before I entered this dingy kitchen, I pressed my ear to the baby's chest again. This time I didn't hear her heart beat. Sweating with panic, I searched in the dark kitchen for milk, or at least water. The odor was revolting. Cold grease, stopped-up sewer, rotten food.... Finally I found a crooked saucepan with a little milk at the bottom. But how old was this milk? One day old and not refrigerated? Although I hated milk, I tasted this one to make sure it wasn't spoiled. I couldn't tell, because milk always tasted terrible to me. As long as it didn't have a sour taste, it was okay, I thought. I found a teaspoon. It was greasy. Unable to find running water to wash it, I rubbed it with my skirt and fed the baby with it. I half filled the spoon with milk and slid one drop down her throat. In the dim light of the candle, sitting on an upside-down bucket, I fed her drop by drop, knowing that she had never been spoon-fed before.

Her eyes were open now and she was strangely quiet. No sucking motions, no wriggling, no wailing or even moaning. She gazed at me with that fixed look of a plastic doll, taking each drop of milk in. My instincts told me that I shouldn't overfeed her. I stopped. But before I could manage to leave the dark kitchen, the glares of many flashlights blinded me.

"Don't move!" A woman ordered. "Take the baby from her," she ordered a guard. "Now handcuff her and bring her to the building."

"The baby was starving. . . " I pleaded.

"You've trespassed. Attempted to escape."

"I didn't. How could I? I'm still inside—"

"This kitchen opens to the street. You were planning to escape."

For the first time I saw an old crooked door at the end of the hut. Behind the door was the street. I could have escaped. I could have been somewhere safe now.

"Leash this Satan worshiper and take her in!" the female guard yelled.

From a back door, they took me inside the building. I didn't see the rituals of the Bathhouse anymore. This door opened to a hallway slightly different than ours. For a moment I thought it was the same corridor. But the cell doors were made of iron here, not wood, and they had a square opening in them, close to the floor. Framed in some of these windows, gloomy faces stared at me. I thought that the prisoners must be lying on the floor to be able to hold their faces to the windows. This hall was the permanents' hall. The corridor was cleaner and every few meters a TV set hung from the ceiling. Because of the blackout the TVs were off, but the same dim yellow bulbs lit the corridor.

One female guard pulled my leash, while two followed me with their machine guns, aiming at my back. They watched me closely, as if with my hands cuffed behind my back, I could draw

a gun and shoot at them. All through the long hallway to the
barred gate, which the Sister with the leash opened with a gigan-
tic key, I thought about the baby. Where had they taken her?

Soon I was sitting in Jamali's room, in the first corridor. This
was the same chair facing the wall. The room was dark, but when
the moon came out of the clouds it shed a dim light through the
small window close to the ceiling. My hands cuffed behind me, I
couldn't look at my watch, but I could feel the long moments pass-
ing. My wrists hurt and the pain kept me awake. I heard the occa-
sional chanting of slogans from the courtyard and the whoop,
whoop, whoop of the whippings. This couldn't still be the hundred lashes of Leila and the young man; they were whipping more
inmates. The program seemed to be long, stretching through the
night.

Then I heard someone snoring, though not loudly. It was a
child's muffled snore. I turned and looked around the room. In the
darkest corner, on the right side of the door, there was a mat on
the floor, a child sleeping on it. It was a boy, sleeping on his belly,
his face turned toward the wall. I watched him for a long time.
This was Ali, Brother Jamali's son. His presence convinced me that
everything was real. I sat for a long time, watching the child.

Finally Ali rolled toward me and opened his eyes. He didn't
move. We stared at each other like two animals—one larger, the
other smaller, the smaller one scared to death, the stronger wounded, not wanting to attack, not intending to harm the smaller one.
They didn't trust each other.

I was the one who broke the silence. I said, "Ali, it's all right.
I'm not a devil. Don't be scared of me."

He didn't even blink.

"Your father is outside in the courtyard. He'll be back soon. Can you go back to sleep?"

He didn't respond. Then I considered the possibility that Jamali's child was deaf and dumb. Without saying anything more, I turned to the wall and waited.

11

"So you want to become a hero, huh? A Mother Teresa or something. Saving babies and shit." Jamali had turned my chair away from the wall and was sitting opposite me. "I'm dead, do you understand? Starved and exhausted. Why should I deal with you now? Don't I deserve to sleep? I haven't been home for forty-eight hours and my son is practically living here. Is this a life I have?" He was asking this from me, not in an angry tone, but a disappointed one. I was a teenager who had misbehaved and was being reproached by her father.

"It's midnight. I need to go home and I won't be back until Sunday. No interrogations tomorrow. Tomorrow is the full moon; I want to take my family to the Holy Hills. Millions of believers will be there, observing His Holy Face. There is a mass prayer. Four million people! Can you take this into your empty head? Can four million be wrong and a handful of shitheads like your brother be right? By the way, your sister-in-law screwed up. Repented. Did you know this? I shouldn't insult her now, she is trying to educate herself!" He sighed, leaned back, and closed his eyes for a second. Sweat beads bubbled on his forehead.

There was a Kerosene lantern on the desk and for the first time I could watch Brother Jamali's face. Hard work and lack of sleep hadn't had any effect on him. His cheeks were red and puffy, his small eyes were hidden in the folds of his flesh, and from his short forehead to his chin and down to his double chin, his face shone with grease. He needed to soap his face, I thought.

"Well, Mother Teresa, all I can tell you is that tonight, with your stupidity, you ruined your own life. I was planning to get rid of you. I was thinking to let you go tomorrow. That's why I didn't take you out tonight. I told myself, Why would I keep this little brat here? Let her sleep and I'll let her go tomorrow." He sighed and stared at me. It was a long pause. Then he said, "I read your journals, by the way. You are really something, mademoiselle— rotten to the core, spoiled, and stupid like all those dirty atheists who fled the country last year. But your brother is another case. He has divorced his class!" Now he burst into such a loud horse-laugh that his son woke up. He sat on the mat, shocked.

"Don't go back to sleep, Ali, we're leaving in few minutes. Home, son. After two days we're heading home. Tomorrow I'm going to take you to the Hills to see the full moon, son. Get up, dear. Find your shoes and let's go."

Ali obeyed, rose, and folded the blanket like a dutiful soldier. Then rubbed his eyes and looked around the room to find his shoes. There was a little hole on his right sock, his toe was sticking out.

"Well, little devil," Brother Jamali stood up and addressed me, "had you stayed a spoiled brat as you came in here last night, I'd let you go tomorrow morning, but since you changed yourself into Mother Teresa, I'm going to keep you here and send you to the permanents' hall. For tonight I guess a little muscle stretch will teach you a good lesson. And the lesson is: don't put your fucking nose in other people's business. It wasn't your goddamn business to take that baby to the kitchen and feed her. Do you know who the baby's father is? The big Satan of the commies. And you fed her." Now he opened the door and called someone in. "Give her a little massage!" Then he held Ali's hand and left the room. But from the hallway he called, "I'll see you in the permanents!"

The hairy female guard and a male guard—the same teenager who was in my house last night, watching me getting dressed—approached me. They removed the handcuffs. I rubbed my wrists immediately.

"Rub them, dear, make them ready for the real massage," the woman told me. They both laughed. "Brother, hold this for me," she gave the handcuffs to the boy. I noticed that she was wearing surgical gloves.

"Mohsen. Call me Mohsen, Sister Soghra."

"How do you know my name?" Sister Soghra asked Mohsen. Her tone wasn't dry and harsh anymore.

"I asked someone." The boy sat on a chair, hung one leg on another in a cool way, looking up at Sister Soghra. He was acting like Clint Eastwood again.

"Don't sit, Brother, I need your help here."

The boy obeyed and stood up. The woman was superior in rank.

"Give me your watch! Who has let you wear this?" she yelled at me.

I took off my watch and looked at it for the last time before I handed it to Sister Soghra.

"Hey, give it to me, I said!" She snapped the watch out of my hand. "Now Brother, I'll pull her arms and you cuff them behind her back, here, under her shoulder blades." She pulled my right arm over my right shoulder, then twisted and stretched my left arm from my waist to my shoulder blades.

"You're breaking my shoulders," I pleaded. "Don't! It hurts!"

"Really?" She said and they both laughed.

"Last night I brought her here," Brother Mohsen boasted. "Rotten people. Pretty soon we'll turn their big house into the Devotee's Headquarters."

"No!" I screamed. The crazy woman was pulling my arms, one from above my shoulder and the other from under my shoulder blades.

"Now!" she said, "Cuff her!"

"I'm trying to—" the boy played with the handcuff behind my back.

Their heads were behind me now and I could hear them gasping. They lingered back there for a long moment. The woman pulled my arms.

"Now!" she said again.

I screamed.

"I'm doing my best, Sister Soghra; you need to pull more."

For a long time they were behind my back, gasping and shouting at each other, prolonging the torment. Finally I heard a "click". I screamed and kept screaming.

12

I opened my eyes in the permanents'. I realized this because of the small square window at the bottom of the iron door. The inmates sat all around the room, side by side. The room was full. But I was lying down, occupying three spaces. I wanted to scratch my head, but I couldn't move my arms. My arms were limp, resting on the floor on either side of my body. Someone bent over me and began to rub them. I smiled at Mrs. Moradi. Her face was still black and blue. She rubbed my upper arm and came all the way down to my fingertips; I didn't feel much. My arms were dead.

"I want to sit up," I said. "I'm okay."

"Shhh," she said.

"What time is it?"

"No one has a watch here, my dear."

"What happened to my watch?"

"I'm sure it's with them. They took it off when they hand-cuffed you."

"Why is everybody so quiet here? Why does no one talk?"

"Shhh . . . rest, dear, rest . . . " and she rubbed my arms again.

Now I tried to look at each prisoner. I started from the first one sitting by the door—a girl my age, maybe even younger. She was also wearing her school uniform. Her two thick, blond braids were out of her scarf, resting on her chest. She had leaned her head back against the wall. Her eyes were closed. Next to her sat an older woman. She was not wearing a scarf. Her hair was colored reddish-blond and showed black at the roots. She rubbed her belly and bit her lips as if she had stomach ache. Next to her Zohre sat, head on her knees, without the baby. Next to Zohre was Leila, her legs stretched in front of her, bandaged from feet to knees. A hooded woman sat next to Leila. In this hot, airless room she had pulled a black stocking over her head and face. She was weaving something with black thread. More stockings, maybe. I looked at her veiled body carefully. This was not Ferial. Ferial was shorter, slimmer. Mrs. Moradi sat above my head and on my left side sat two more women. One wore round eye-glasses with thick lenses. She looked young but a patch of gray hair hung out of her black scarf. The last woman was much older. She resembled the gray-haired woman. They sat head to head, whispering.

I closed my eyes and thought about this silence. If the hooded person stayed here, we could never talk. I tried to remember something pleasant, to entertain myself. But my head itched and I couldn't scratch it. I wished someone would wash my hair with warm water and plenty of shampoo. I remembered when every now and then my mother took me to her hair dresser and the woman lay my head back on the headrest and shampooed it with warm water. How good it felt. But it never lasted long enough. I always wanted more, for a longer time.

So I lay there this way, thinking about my immediate needs. I asked myself, What if a jinni appeared and asked me to make three wishes, but none could be freedom? The first one would be to move my arms; the second, to wash my hair; and the third wish would be to eat. I was hungry. It seemed that I had missed a couple of meals. I also wished I knew how much time had passed since they cuffed my wrists behind my back. Was it the same day, or the next day?

I was dozing again when suddenly the red-haired woman bounced up and leaped toward me like a wild leopard.

"You bastard! You son of a bitch! It's all because of you! You're doing this to me and my baby! Death on you! Plague and black death!"

I sat up, trying to hide myself behind Mrs. Moradi, who held her arms around me for protection. But the woman was not attacking me, she was looking up on the wall. Everybody looked up and saw a picture of the Great Leader hanging close to the ceiling. It was a color picture cut from a magazine, taped to the wall with two pieces of transparent tape.

"Sit down, Robab!"

"He is responsible for my baby, this bastard!"

"Sit down!"

This was Leila, ordering the crazy woman to sit down. It seemed that I had missed something here. When and how had Leila gotten to know this woman so well as to be able to order her to do something? And the red-haired woman obeyed Leila. She sat down, rubbing her belly again. Now she just murmured with herself.

"No one believes me," she said with tears in her eyes. "There is a baby in my belly. It's six months old. But next to it there is a little machine—the size of a clock radio. The machine controls the baby's growth. Now the poor thing has been controlled for a long time. Very long. It's not healthy. The damn thing shouldn't keep controlling my baby's growth. I'm thankful for the machine, though. What if I'd have my labor here? What would happen to me...?"

"They don't have a psychiatric wing here," Mrs. Moradi whispered to me. "They mix the sane with the insane. Thank God Leila can handle her. If it wasn't for her, she would attack someone."

I noticed that this room had two windows, exactly like the first cell in the temporary. One close to the ceiling and one close to the floor, opening to the courtyard. Both windows were painted white. Through the paint I could see the shadow of the bars outside. Now the repentant sat in front of the lower window, blocking it. If she weren't sitting there and if the window were not painted, I could see the courtyard—a tree trunk, maybe, pigeons pecking on the brick floor.

When the light dimmed behind the two windows, someone came in and called the repentant out. Then they slid trays of food inside the room from the window in the door. We rushed to the trays, but Leila told us to hold on. We needed to move our bodies. She said now that the Raven was out—that's what the inmates called the hooded repentants—we should exercise. She was herself sitting, her legs bandaged up to her knees. But she gave us instructions to stand in the middle of the cell in two circles and walk in opposite directions. She kept counting and clapping her hands in rhythm. Robab enjoyed herself, laughing loudly. She forgot the baby and the machine.

"Now run in place! One, two, one, two.... Now hop. One, one, one, one.... Now walk fast, one circle to the right, one to the left."

Someone began to sing. All the women joined in:

The sun is rising
the flowers blooming
Spring is coming, spring is coming!

13

I sat by the painted window, legs folded into my chest. The silence was heavy. Everybody was sleeping. There was not enough room for me to lie down. After we came back from the toilet and the lights went out, we all lay down to sleep. Once I sat up to turn to my other side and someone in the dark stretched herself out and occupied my place. Now I squeezed my body into a ball and sat next to the window. I didn't want to wake anyone. Tomorrow I could sleep in a wider space.

My arms were coming back to life. I felt pain and Leila said that this was a good sign. I moved my fingers to exercise them. Then I began to play with the window. I scratched the paint with my thumb nail. A piece came off. I knew how dangerous this was, but I kept scratching the paint. It was a compulsive act. Uncontrollable. Crazy. I knew that I should stop scratching the glass, but I kept doing it. I wanted to see outside. This was what I kept telling myself.

The moon was full tonight. I remembered that only a few months ago at this time people partied on the roofs. The revolution was still new, the whole city was festive. There was a high-rise in our neighborhood that had been an office building, but now more than one hundred families occupied the building's rooms. The roof of this high-rise was the liveliest in the city. People brought folding tables up there and covered them with food and drinks. Believers and nonbelievers sat in friendly groups, talking until morning. Their discussions were not just about the existence or non-existence of the sacred face on the moon, but was about the destiny of the revolution, the upcoming elections, and the function of the new government. Activists, like my brother, shuffled themselves among the tenants to do mass work, to educate people and analyze the situation for them. One evening, walking back home from the market, I urged Mali to let us go there and join the gathering, but she forbade me to even get close to the high-rise.

In a short while, half of the paint and half of my thumbnail were gone. I bent my head and saw the courtyard's brick floor— old brick, narrow and reddish-brown. This was the courtyard of the old bathhouse, but I couldn't tell if it was close to the kitchen. Now I knew that the kitchen had a door to the street. I was close to it that night, with Zohre's baby in my arms. But even if I had noticed the door, I wouldn't have been able to make a decision. I could not escape with someone else's baby, nor could I have left her in the dark kitchen alone.

Sitting in the silence looking out from the window, I heard distant sounds of people cheering, or maybe children screaming with joy. This sound came from the right. It was a happy uproar and continued for a while, then it stopped. Now I heard the siren of the blackout in the distance. The happy uproar didn't come from the Holy Hills. The Hills were outside the city and the prayers or chants of the devotees were far from cheerful.

Listening and watching like a wild animal in the heart of the night, I noticed a shadow on the moonlit brick floor. I bent to see better. It was the lower part of a woman's body, the long skirt of her black chador; she passed from one side—the wall of this building—to the other side, where I couldn't see. She dragged a sack behind her. The sack was heavy. Once she stopped right behind the window, turned toward the sack, grabbed the top with both hands, pulled it with effort, and walked backwards. When she bent to grab the sack, I saw half of her face in the moonlight. Her chador and the black scarf under it had slipped down on her shoulders. I saw her hair. She had henna-colored hair pressed to her scalp. Then I noticed one long eyebrow, the shape of an Arabian dagger, stretching to the edge of her temple.

Next morning while I was dizzy with sleep, hanging on Mrs. Moradi in the toilet line, Soghra, the hairy guard, pulled me out of the line, leashed me, and dragged me into the long hallway. We passed through a barred gate that separated the temporaries' and the permanents' halls. Soghra didn't blindfold me. I saw numerous new faces in the temporaries' hall. Men and women, weary and wounded, stood or lay on the floor. They were in the same condition that I had been the first day.

Jamali was waiting for me in his room.

"Sit down!" he ordered.

I sat, looking around to find Ali. But he wasn't there.

"Congratulations Mother Teresa, you did a great job. Served us well."

My heart banged in my chest and throat and even in my mouth. For some unknown reason, I felt more scared than at any time before. What had I done to serve them?

"You can't guess? You killed the baby. You poisoned the

Satan's seed. Thank you!"

He was standing above me and I couldn't see his sweaty face, but I could smell cold grease on him and hear the hissing sound of his breath. Still I didn't understand.

"Did you hear me? The milk was spoiled. You killed Zohre's baby. Now go and tell her what you did. Get up!"

I didn't get up. I couldn't.

"Get up, I told you!" He pulled the leash that was still hanging off me and lifted me up. The chair fell with a bang. He pulled me farther up. I was on my toes. He was choking me. "Have courage, little devil. Go back to your cell and tell your friend that you poisoned her baby. Tell her that you're a murderer. Off now, you dirty little rat!"

I had missed the toilet and breakfast. The women sat around the room, with the Raven weaving her black stocking among them. I noticed that Mrs. Moradi was sitting in front of the window, covering the paintless pane with her big body. When I squeezed myself next to her, she gave me a reproachful look, pointing with her eyes to the window. She was scolding me soundlessly.

But I wasn't even thinking about the window. Let them find out that I scratched the paint off. Let them whip me in the empty pool. Let them shoot me.

For the first time since my arrest, I wished for death.

14

I was lying down, pretending to be asleep, but I was listening to Robab laughing, having a monologue:

"Yes, sir. It's the size of a clock radio. No sir, I haven't seen it. I was unconscious when they installed the machine in my belly—"

"Get up girls, they're coming to your cell any minute now." A young guard, Sister Soghra's assistant, told us through the tray window. "They're coming to investigate."

I sat up. All the women were pulling their chadors onto their heads, getting ready for the investigator. Mrs. Moradi pulled me toward her.

"Let's stand in front of this window and cover it. If they notice the paint is gone, God knows what they'll do to us."

We all stood around the room. Zohre was still missing. For the first time, I noticed that the older lady who always whispered with the younger gray-haired woman could not stand on her own. She didn't seem to be more than fifty-five, but her back was bent. The younger woman held her up.

"Poor woman," Mrs. Moradi whispered to me. "Spine injury. She needs to be in the hospital. Thank God her daughter is with her. They arrested them together."

"Why?" I asked. I was sleepy and confused.

"The daughter is a university professor. She had a trunk full of books. God knows what kind of books. But that's her job, isn't it? She teaches. She and her mother were driving. The guards stopped their car and searched. They found the books and brought them here."

"Why?"

Mrs. Moradi looked deep into my eyes. "Are you all right, child? What happened in Jamali's room this morning? You came back and didn't say a word. Then you fell asleep. What happened?"

"The baby—"

"Which baby, dear?"

But before I could say more, the door was flung open and Brother Jamali came in with a robed man. I recognized the clergy immediately. He was the short chubby man who led the prayers in the bathhouse the night before, encouraging the prisoners to repent.

"Agha is here today to investigate," Jamali said, "to see if the prisoners need something—"

"We need a fan." Leila raised her voice. "The heat is intolerable."

"Shut your mouth and don't let me insult you in front of a holy person," Jamali yelled at Leila. "You cannot demand anything. I'll make sure that you don't get anything. Arrogant whore!"

"Let them talk, Brother Jamali," the robed man said gently. "I'm here to listen to the complaints. Is there anything else you need besides a fan?"

"We need to take a shower. There are lice in the cell. It's unhealthy; dirtiness is against the laws of religion," Mrs. Moradi said.

"How long is it that these ladies haven't washed?"

"Most of them have been here for less than a week. Shower time is once a week. Every Friday, sir. They have to wait a couple of days more. And I'll see about the lice."

"Anything else?" Agha asked.

"My mother can barely stand up or sit down. She needs to see a doctor," the professor said.

"How did this happen, Brother Jamali?" Agha asked innocently.

"How did it happen? People come here with their own diseases. This lady came with a bad back."

"This is not true. My mother was healthy. She was beaten up. A respectable lady was beaten up—"

"You're lying, Madame and here liars get punished. I won't forget this lie," Jamali interrupted her. He was panting. "If you have anything else, tell Agha, but don't waist his precious time."

"The machine, sir, what if it starts to work?" Robab burst out. "What the hell am I going do if the baby grows?"

"What is this woman saying?" Agha asked.

"She is a looney," Jamali knocked on his temple and laughed.

"Is she political?"

"Oh, yes, sir. They found her walking in the streets without a veil, talking to herself, insulting the Great leader and spitting at the His Holy pictures. Can she be more political than that?"

"That is outrageous. If she keeps babbling, take her to solitary confinement," Agha instructed.

When they turned to leave, Leila who was the only one sitting on the floor, her bandaged legs stretched out in front of her, shouted, "We need a fan!" The door slammed and clicked.

A short while later, Soghra and her assistant, a small female guard with beautiful blue eyes, came in with scissors. One by one they took us to the middle of the room, and made us kneel on the floor. They cut our hair above our necks and said this was to reduce the lice. Friday, someone would come to shave our heads.

Roya, the girl with blond braids, resisted. Like a six-year-old, she grabbed her braids in her fists and shook her head no. Soghra and the blue-eyed girl dragged her to the middle of the floor and forced her onto her knees.

"Leave her alone," Leila said. "She is not feeling well."

"This is an order," Soghra said. "This bitch wants to keep her pretty hair. Everybody must shave Friday. You devils have brought filth and lice with you. We're trying to clean you."

The small guard held Roya's head from behind and Soghra placed her scissors at the root of her thick braid and snapped it with one sharp click. She did the same with the other braid. The girl touched the end of her uprooted braids, now sticking out from behind her ears like strange horns, and burst into hysterical sobs. She was crying as if her whole life depended on her braids.

15

After the haircut they took Mrs. Moradi out. She was gone for several hours and missed her dinner. I sat in front of the small window, motionless. No one besides Mrs. Moradi had noticed that the paint was gone.

Since the day they handcuffed me and took my watch away, I hadn't known the time. The weakness or strength of the light behind the windows and the degree of heat, which I could tell by pressing my hand on the windowpane, told me the approximate time.

Sometime after dinner and before the blackouts, they took us out to the corridor and ordered us to sit on the floor in front of the hanging TV. The set was close to the ceiling and we had to tilt our heads back to see the screen. Soghra explained that the program we were about to watch was the repentants' confessions and would take one hour.

Men with a few days' growth of beard, women with black veils appeared one by one in front of the video camera to confess. Their faces were stony, their sentences choppy, and their voices mechanical and monotonous. They had no soul in them.

"Here I confess that I have been a follower of a satanic ideology. I was young and I didn't know the right path. I was deceived by the spies of the East and the West. I forgot The Almighty and the Holy Faith. Now I repent and plead forgiveness from the Holy

Leader whose sacred face appears on the white surface of the moon—"

".... I'm ready to cooperate with the Devotees of the Holy Revolution. I want to serve my Leader and my Faith by naming the corrupt elements who scheme for the destruction of our young Holy Republic ... I beg forgiveness from our Holy benevolent Leader whose face is carved by the Lord on the full moon—"

All the tones the same, the expressions the same, and the texts almost the same. I counted them: twenty-four repentants. The last one was Ferial, my sister-in-law. She repeated the same thing.

That night I lay on my back next to the paintless window and pulled the black chador over my body and raised my knees. This way I made myself into a big black hill and covered the glass. Neither Mrs. Moradi nor Zohre showed up. My cellmates whispered for a while and the Raven kept saying, "hush!" until everybody was quiet.

I listened to the silence and heard the same burst of laughter, children's cheerful screams, and hubbub of sounds that I heard the other night come from the outside. Then I looked out to see if that strange woman was going to appear with another heavy sack. For a long time I stared at the courtyard's moonlit brick floor and waited. The woman didn't come. Instead an old man ran barefoot on the brick floor, hunching to grab something. A small animal slipped inside the bushes. The old man chased it with cupped hands, trying to catch it.

A short while later, I sat up with horror. I thought that I dreamed about a baby sucking my breast. I thought that I heard the distinct noise of munching and muffled gurgling in the baby's throat. I looked around, removed the chador to let the moonlight flow in. Everybody lay on the floor, side by side—sardines in a can. Robab snored like a man. The lady with the bad back moaned. The high school girl, Roya, rested her head on Leila's shoulder. In the moonlight she looked like a sulking baby. The ends of her crookedly cut braids stuck out from under her ears like an animal's horns. At the other wall, Zohre lay down with her baby. She was awake, breast feeding her daughter.

I couldn't breathe. Rubbing my eyes and chewing my lips hard to make sure that I was awake, I found my way among the bodies, and crawled toward Zohre. Her large white breast was out, held in the baby's tiny hands. The baby was patting the breast with joy, scratching it, fingering it, pinching it, all the while making gurgling and munching sounds.

"She is alive!" I whispered.

"She was with me all yesterday and she is going to stay with me forever."

"How come?"

She lowered her voice and said, "I'm just telling you, please don't tell the others. I've decided to cooperate. I can't lose my baby. Maybe this is my weakness. Maybe someone else would be stronger. But I can't live without her."

"You want to repent?"

"Yes."

"They won't leave you alone, then. You'll have to wear that black stocking all day and spy on the others. You may have to whip or even kill your own husband."

"My husband is dead. He was among the first eighty. I don't want to lose my baby, too. I'll raise her. Who knows? Maybe things change."

"I'm so happy she's alive!"

"Why shouldn't she be? I fed her all day yesterday. She's such a glutton! I washed her too. She's as fresh and healthy as a rose."

"She is a rose."

"For real, she is. That's her name."

"Are you serious?"

"Yes. My husband named her Rosa. After Rosa Luxemburg."

"A movie star?"

"No, dummy. A revolutionary!" Zohre laughed at my ignorance.

16

The next morning after breakfast, Baba, the old janitor, who was sick for the past few days, brought a fan and planted it in the middle of the room. I recognized him. This was the old man who was chasing something in the dark last night. He was bald, thin, and short, his back stooped. He was missing most of his teeth and his remaining teeth were strangely long and yellow like some animal's fangs. But he was friendly, and called us "girls" all the time.

"Well, girls, here is your fan. Let it turn around and circulate the air. It's damn hot here, like the hell itself. Outside the heat is melting the asphalt. People are desperate. But poor animals are doing worse. I saw a donkey carrying watermelons. He stopped in the middle of the alley and didn't move anymore. The donkey man whipped him. The animal didn't move. Finally the donkey passed out and all the watermelons rolled into the street. Most of them broke and became food for the ants and flies. The donkey never stood up again and the donkey man sat there crying. That's a street scene for you. The heat is hell's heat. They say there is a cholera epidemic on the battlefields."

Baba stayed for a while, adjusting the fan and talking. Women talked with him. They asked him questions about outside.

"What do people know about this place, Baba?" Leila asked.

"About here? Well they know it exists. This bathhouse has existed since the time of the old king. It's more than a century old.

My grandfather and my father were janitors here."

"Do people know what goes on here?" Leila insisted.

"They know and they don't. They know and they don't want to know—if you understand my meaning. Well, I have to go now. Just slide your trays out. I'll pick them up. Friday afternoon you'll all have visitation. Cheer up girls!"

This old man looked like all the janitors I'd ever known in my life. The janitors of the girls' high school were toothless and talkative too. They enjoyed gathering the girls around them, telling them strange stories. I thought about the old man for a while— born in the prison, working in the prison all his life, no matter to which government it belonged.

Then I thought about the visitation, about Mali. Maybe my uncles would come with her. No, they wouldn't. They wouldn't set foot in such a place. It was not good for their reputation. They had already become cold to our family because of Hamid's activism, and because once Hamid called them "fossils." They were monarchists, sitting in the darkness of their thickly curtained living rooms on layers of silk carpets, waiting for the king's son to grow up, return from his hiding place, and save them. I didn't want them to visit me.

Would Hamid and Ferial be in the visitation with me? Hamid maybe, but not Ferial.

I would never cry in front of Mali. I'd smile and tell her that I was doing fine. I just wished I could wash before the visitation. I didn't want to look horrible. I hadn't seen myself in a mirror for four days. I knew that I had greasy hair sticking to my scalp, now cut short in a crooked way. I knew that my teeth were yellow and my face was pale. My eyes were red and sunken, my clothes dirty and smelly; dry blood had stained them. My wrists were black and blue and maybe my face was bruised too, from the rubber rulers. Seeing me, Mali would scream. I closed my eyes, dreaming about soap and water.

Midday they opened the door and let Mrs. Moradi in. Half of her face was bandaged. A whiplash ran diagonally from her left temple to her right cheek beneath the bandage. I rushed to her, helping her to sit down next to me. She moaned faintly. Her lips were cracked. She was thirsty. We gave her some cold tea left over from our breakfast that we had hidden in a paper cup. Then we helped her to lie down. She closed the eye that was not covered by the bandage.

The fan rotated to the right, then to the left. It made me sleepy to look at it. Some women slept all day. The professor—I knew now that her name was Dr. Mina—was murmuring something to herself. It was poetry. I liked that gray lock of hair hanging out of her scarf. I liked her quiet and reserved manner and the way she always managed to look clean. I looked at her with admiration.

"Can you say it louder?" I asked. "My father used to read poetry for us. I love to listen."

"It's amazing how my memory is bringing these forgotten lines back to me. I learned these poems in my early youth, when I was a college student."

"Are you really a professor?"

She laughed. "What a big deal! Anybody can be. I'm a teacher. I teach at the university."

"My father was a professor, too. He taught philosophy. What

do you teach?"

"Political science. Government."

"Oh. This must be something they don't want you to teach."

"They don't want women to teach anything, period," she said. "But let me recite this poem for you. Mother, you listen too. You'll remember it."

Her mother, who lay on her side, raised her head and said, "Go on, I'm with you. I'm sorry I can't sit up. This damned back hurts."

"Stay with us.

Don't sink to the bottom," Dr. Mina murmured with her soft, even voice,

"like a fish going to sleep.

Be with the ocean moving steadily all night,

Not scattered like a rainstorm.

The spring we're looking for

Is somewhere in this murkiness.

Seethe nightlights up there travelingtogether,

The candle awake in its gold dish.

Don't slide into the cracks of ground like spilled mercury.

When the full moon comes out, look around."

17

We were at my uncle's beach house. Everybody else was inside, playing cards, because it was a cloudy day. I was outside, strolling on the beach, drawing shapes on the sand with a long stick. Then I dragged the stick behind me, making a long line. Papa followed the line and found me. He took the stick and wrote something on the sand. I couldn't make out what it was. I wrote something, too. For a while we wrote words on the sand without talking to each other. But I couldn't read his words. It was a strange kind of conversation. Then a huge wave came and washed the words away. We laughed. Now, without any introduction, Papa read a poem for me. The poem was about someone who went to the sea and spent the whole night with the boatman. The boatman sang in such a way that when the man returned to land, he kept dreaming about the sea. After the poem, Papa walked toward the water, stepped into it and broke the waves open. He walked and walked until he became a tiny spot. Then he sank and I didn't see him anymore.

18

The nights that the Raven didn't sleep in our cell we sat up late and talked in whispers. Rumors were exchanged, gossip, stories, fantasies. These were ordinary women, after all. None were a professional activist, a militant, a guerilla fighter, or a politician. Even Dr. Mina, who taught political science, only dealt with books. She had never done anything beyond speaking. Neither had Leila, who was a surgeon and didn't even know much about political parties. Mrs. Moradi was just a mother who was being punished because of her son. We didn't know much about Roya, but she was too timid and withdrawn to be an activist. Robab's case was obviously ridiculous. Zohre was probably the most political of all, but she was missing now. After she told me that she had decided to repent, she and her baby disappeared.

So we sat and gossiped. We exchanged the news we had heard in the toilet lines, in the interrogation rooms, from Baba, or someone from the next cell. Leila had heard that they raped the virgins before execution. Because if they killed them as virgins, they'd send them straight to heaven. They wanted to send them to hell. We talked about this rumor for a long time. Dr. Mina believed that this was impossible, such a crime could never happen. It would cause international reaction; the United Nations would intervene. We all laughed when she mentioned the United Nations.

Then Mrs. Moradi said that she had heard about a girl who

hadn't peed for a week, her belly had swelled like a pregnant woman and they were taking her to the hospital to attach a hose to her bladder. She screamed with pain and tore her face with her nails. Now Leila protested as a doctor. She said this was medically impossible. Not urinating for a week was definitely an exaggeration.

After these horror stories Dr. Mina's mother, who was older than everyone and was quiet all the time, said, "Don't you have a good story to tell, you women? Should we suffer all day and then listen to these horrible tales all night? Tell us some nice stories, with happiness and a glimpse of hope."

We all nodded. Leila hugged her and apologized. We each sat and thought deep and hard to find a happy story. A few minutes passed.

Suddenly Robab broke the silence and said, "Once I had a husband; he was very handsome. His name was Jahan. Tall and strong, an adventurous man. He was a young merchant, traveled to Turkey and Arabia all the time, buying and selling silk and perfumes. I had a room full of silk garments and colorful bottles of perfume. But I never wore them because Jahan was never around."

She kept quiet and started to pat her belly, rubbing it as if it hurt.

"Then what?" we asked.

"Nothing. I can't make a sad story into a happy one. I just can't. This baby reminds me of him." She burst into tears. "He planted this baby and left me. He went to Turkey and never returned. Then I went to a doctor and he installed this machine in my belly to stop the baby from growing. But it keeps growing and growing. The machine must be broken." Robab was wailing now.

"Let's sleep now. We may have a hard day tomorrow," Leila said, to control Robab's hysteria. We all lay down to sleep. Robab wept for a long time.

19

In the shower, Mrs Moradi pulled a plastic bag over her head to protect her bandaged face. Leila wore two garbage bags on her legs. They looked grotesque, aliens from outer space. We laughed at them. The laughter became contagious, hysterical. We laughed so much that our bellies hurt. Robab peed on herself.

Dr. Mina spent her whole shower time washing her mother, who couldn't bend, or raise her arms. Shower time was short. If we didn't rush, we wouldn't get clean. The soap was the cheap kind and smelled nasty—nothing like the scent of the soap in my bathing daydreams. It smelled of the kind of soap my grand-mother's maid used to wash the laundry. That was long ago, when I was little and sat in the yard, watching the laundry lady rubbing dirty clothes with a huge yellow brick of soap. Grandmother believed that the American detergents, which were everywhere in the market, couldn't clean her clothes as well as those smelly bricks.

Although the soap was nasty, I used plenty of it to wash my hair and body. There were no walls between the five showers, and some women who were shy washed themselves with their under-wear on. Robab screamed with joy like a child and sang a vulgar song: "If I wriggle my butt here, he complains . . . if I wriggle my butt there, he still complains—" and she wriggled her fat butt. It seemed that she had forgotten all about her baby and the controlling machine.

After ten minutes Soghra blew a whistle and the water stopped. Some of us stayed with soapsuds in our hair and faces. We begged Soghra to open the water for just a few more seconds, but she didn't. She gave each of us a towel and told us to keep it clean. It was the prison's property. And then she gave us identical black uniforms, large black scarves, wide black chadors, and a pair of black rubber slippers that were too large, men's sizes. The guards took our own clothes and shoes from us.

Now in our black uniforms, looking like penguins in single file, we walked toward our cell. But someone was screaming. We heard slaps and smacks on bare skin. We turned and saw Roya still standing under the dry shower, rubbing her body as if washing it. There was no water, but she kept doing the pantomime. Soghra and two other female guards were trying to pull her out of the shower area. They slapped her face and her naked body. They had rubber gloves on and the slaps sounded muffled and reddened her skin. But Roya kept screaming, "I'm not clean yet. I'm not clean—"

Seeing the guards busy with Roya, Mrs. Moradi, who was behind me in line, told me in a whisper that all day yesterday they had hanged her son upside down from the ceiling and had forced her to watch. Finally she couldn't tolerate it and rushed toward her son to bring him down. That's when they whipped her face.

"'What do you want to know, huh?' I yelled at them. 'Bring him down and I'll tell you what you want.'"

"Did they bring him down?"

"They did. But he had passed out. They're going to call me

again when he comes to."

"What do they want from you?"

"Names, my dear. Names of my son's friends. I know my boy. He'll die and won't say a word. If he doesn't break, I won't."

"And if he does?"

"Still I won't." Mrs. Moradi smiled with her swollen lips and squeezed my shoulder.

20

In the middle of our cell, Jamali and another man were waiting for us. This man was middle-aged and short with a thin mustache above his lip. He had on a khaki shirt and his khaki pants were tucked into military boots. The minute we entered, Jamali hollered.

"I shouldn't have let you bitches take a shower. Brother Hosseini is here to take you to the barn. That 's were you belong."

"Why don't you kill us and get rid of us, huh?" Mrs. Moradi burst out. "What is this constant play-game here? We are sick and tired of this!" She was beside herself.

"Sick and tired? I'm going to show you who is sick and tired. Look at this!" He pointed to the floor. The picture of the Great Leader was on the floor. "You have thrown the holy picture of the Great Leader on the floor. You have to get punished for this."

"The fan has blown it," Leila said. "It was taped to the wall."

"You shut up. If there is one person in this facility I want to kill with my own hands, it's you."

"What have I done to you, Jamali?" Leila said. "I'm the prey, you're the hunter. I'm in your hands. Why are you afraid of me?"

"Afraid? Of a whore like you? I'll show you who is afraid. Taking the Leader's picture down is inciting riot. Brother Hosseini will take care of you. They're all yours, Hosseini, take them to the barn. I'm done with them." He left the cell and slammed the door, as if sulking after a domestic quarrel.

Brother Hosseini who looked like a military man but didn't have any of those moons and stars hanging on his shirt pocket, smiled and drew a long leather whip out from somewhere. He slashed the cement floor. Whoop!

"All in a single file! Right hand on the shoulder of the person in front. Blindfold them, Sister."

Sister Soghra and her assistant, the short girl with beautiful eyes, rushed toward us, fished in their deep uniform pockets and took black kerchiefs out. Before they blindfolded me I glanced at the small paintless window behind Hosseini's legs. It was dusk outside.

"If you talk to each other, you'll receive a lash. Understood?" Hosseini said with the hoarse voice and rough tone of a military commander.

"My mother cannot walk. She has a back injury," Dr. Mina said.

"I'm sure she can make herself walk if she has to. We don't provide stretchers here. Move now. Hurry up!"

We moved in darkness. The shoulder I was touching was Leila's. I squeezed it gently. She gave it a little playful jerk.

21

Who knew if this was really a barn? I didn't smell animals, hay, cow shit, or horse sweat. When they pulled us out of the van, we walked with our rubber slippers on dirt. I could feel the dirt and dust getting inside the open toes of my large slippers, soiling my clean feet.

"Stop here," Hosseini ordered. "Spread them out, Sister."

Soghra and the blue eyed girl pulled our arms, dragging us in different directions. They stood us in a distance from one another.

"Now stand here till morning. The van will come and get you at six o'clock. There are a dozen armed repentants standing around you, guarding you, and my office is right here, facing the barn. If you sit, they'll shoot you. Understood?"

He left. We heard footsteps on the sand.

"But I can't stand all night, the machine will stop working. The baby will grow!" Robab pleaded.

"Shut her up!" Hosseini's voice came from a distance.

I heard smacks and slaps. Robab shrieked.

"Don't beat me! Why do you beat me? What have I done, huh? Is it a crime to be pregnant?"

More slaps and kicks. I felt the presence of several people around her, beating her.

"If she keeps bitching, bring her here. I'll hang her up all night till her baby comes out of her mouth," Hosseini yelled from a farther distance, as if on the other side of a courtyard.

"Stand up now!" Soghra ordered Robab. "Either you stand here, or he'll hang you upside down. Which one do you want, huh?"

"I'll stand here," Robab said, weeping. "I'll stand."

"And keep your mouth shut till morning."

"Yes, Ma'am."

I had a feeling that this place had no roof. The night's dewdrops sat on my face and hands. I felt the moisture. And I felt the presence of the moon. It must have been a chipped saucer again, getting less and less round, preparing for a long absence. I breathed. I could breathe. I kept telling myself that I could breathe. They hadn't taken this from me, yet. I took deep breaths and the air was fresh as if this place was not a barn and I was standing in an open field like a tree and the moon was floating over me and the night was wrapping its friendly gown, an azure silk, around my body. The veins in my calves burned and my soles hurt, but I could breathe.

Now I heard a thud. Someone fell. I heard the guards, or the repentants, those who were watching us, rushing to the fallen person. They slapped her.

"She's passed out—"

"Make sure she is not pretending—"

"Mother!" Dr. Mina called.

"Shut up, or I'll shoot you!" A man said.

I realized that we were being watched by men, too. Men and women. These guards were staying up all night, watching us standing. I smiled. Then I laughed. Soundlessly. Inside my chest. I laughed because the guards were being tortured with us.

These were the things I tried not to think about: Leila and her injured feet. Mrs. Moradi and her heavy body. And also my brother—if he was still alive. Now I realized that since the first day I had tried to push Hamid's image out of my mind. Maybe I was afraid that he might have been among the first eighty. But now he kept creeping into my head. His face, his dark curly hair, his slightly slanted eyes. My mother called him "my little Chinese prince!" Then I tried to reject the possibility that Ferial could be one of the guards watching us tonight.

When I lifted one foot up someone shouted, "Put your foot down." They were watching us closely and the night was moving slowly. It was just the first hour; many hours were to come. Now someone played with the tuner of a transistor radio and fixed it on a station. Religious lamentations filled the air. It was distracting. I lost track of my thoughts. I couldn't think with this monotonous sound. Then I heard another thud and I was sure that this was Mrs. Moradi. I was happy for her. They dragged her out.

I thought that the bastard who turned the radio on did this on purpose to cover the sounds of the night. He didn't want us to enjoy the little noises of nature. Whenever the religious chant would stop, I could hear the frogs and the sudden crescendo of the crickets. We were out in the open air. I had no doubt now. There was no barn. We were standing under the vast sky like tall trees, dew drops sitting on us. Billions of stars were above us, watching us, winking at us, telling us that standing all night with our eyes closed was not a torture, it was what trees did all the time.

My scattered thoughts circled and circled and finally linked the stars to my brother, Hamid. I remembered when I was ten and Hamid was twenty-two, he picked me up from summer school everyday in Papa's car. I adored him and sat erect in the car so that all my classmates could see me with my handsome grown-up brother. I remembered that once when he picked me up, I was injured. I had fallen from the swing and my knees were bandaged by the school nurse and now after a few hours the bruises were burning as if they were on fire. I cried in the car and Hamid tried to calm me down. He stopped and bought me ice cream, but I didn't feel better. Finally he took me home. My parents were out, so he and Mali took me to the clinic. The nurse put some kind of ointment on my knees that felt very cold and instantly killed the pain.

It was a hot summer and Papa hadn't installed air-conditioners yet. Most nights we slept on top of the roof. The roof had been paved with asphalt. We sprinkled some water on the hot asphalt, so that the dust would settle and the floor would cool off. Then we opened our folding beds and raised the mosquito nets like big tents around our beds. I remember that I was lying that night under the mosquito net, reading, when Hamid called me out. He took my hand and led me to the edge of the roof. He said, "Look up!" I looked up and saw billions of stars crowding the sky, hanging in the dark. It was strange. I hadn't seen the sky so full before.

He said, "Do you remember your pain this afternoon?"

I said, "Yes."

He said, "Whenever I have a bad pain, or a serious problem, I just think about the universe. How vast it is. And how small I am.

And how very tiny my problem is. Then I feel much better. Then I feel that I don't have a problem at all."

Wherever Hamid was, if he was alive, he was thinking about the stars. So was I.

"I did it! Shoot me! Shoot me! I took the picture down!"

I heard the guards rushing toward the voice. It was Roya. She was panting, screaming, and pleading with them to shoot her.

"I swear to God. It was me. I took the picture of the Leader down. Because I hate him. I hate him. I hate him—" and she broke into a violent sob.

They beat her. But she screamed the same things. They kept beating her until she became quiet. Then I heard Brother Hosseini's sleepy voice approaching our area.

"What the hell is going on here, huh? I was trying to get a couple of hours of sleep. What did you do to her? Did you kill her?"

"No, Brother," a man said. "She insulted the Great Leader—"

"Take her out. She's either dead or passed out. Is this the way you watch these bastards? If Brother Jamali wanted to kill them, he wouldn't need you and me here. He could take care of it himself. I don't want to hear any noise anymore. I'm fucking tired and I want to sleep."

He left and I heard the guards dragging Roya's body on the sand. Someone turned the damned radio off.

I was left alone with the sounds of the night. I smiled, then laughed inside my chest and listened carefully so as not to miss a single, tiny sound. Then I thought I heard the distant sweep of waves pouring one on another, sliding toward the shore. A roar, then sweep, then slide, now silence. In the darkness I saw my father, his gray mustache and beard, a faint smile on his peaceful face, his left eye slightly smaller than the right because of so many hours of reading, pressing his right temple, squinting. It was rainy and we were standing on the shore. With a long stick in my hand, I wrote something on the wet sand. Papa took the stick from me and wrote a few words. We laughed. A huge tide washed away the words. Papa walked toward the sea.

22

When they took us back to the cell and removed the blindfolds, we were only three, Dr. Mina, Leila, and I. Mina's mother, Mrs. Moradi, and Roya had passed out. I wasn't sure what had happened to Robab. When Soghra slammed the door and locked it, Dr. Mina fell on the cement floor, sobbing. We didn't talk to each other that morning. We slept. I dreamed about standing on a shore for a long time, until the end of the world, trying to find the meaning of what my father had written on the sand.

When we opened our eyes the cell was full.

We didn't know anyone anymore. Leila, Dr. Mina, and I squeezed together next to the door, leaving more than enough room for the ten new women. A Raven sat under the picture of the Leader, now secured with four big nails. She wove black stockings. I had lost track of time. I didn't know what day it was or how long ago we'd spent a night standing up. The small, paintless window was now behind the inmates who were sitting against the wall. Once when one of them bent over, I saw the dark night.

We hadn't had a meal for a long time and my stomach hurt. A sharp knife pierced a spot under my chest bones; the knife turned and swirled my insides. The fan wasn't in the room anymore. They had taken it away to make room for more people. The heat, the dense air, and the foul odor of so many unwashed bodies brought my insides into my mouth many times.

After a bite of dinner, which was the usual amount of rice and lentil, but now for ten more people, they took us to the corridor to watch the confessions. We were happy to be able to stretch out and sit more comfortably on the corridor's cool cement floor. This was a luxury. A nice breeze blew from somewhere, fresh and soothing. I kept my face turned in that direction and closed my eyes.

Among the many men and women who appeared on the screen and confessed, I recognized Zohre. There was a brief eye contact between Leila and me. Leila's eyes were sad.

"Now I believe in the Faith and The Great Leader of the Holy Revolution. Now I wait for the next full moon, the honor of observing His Sacred Image —"

Back in the cell, we found Robab and Mrs. Moradi sitting there. Happy to have them back, we hugged them. Robab said that she had her best sleep in the clinic and her baby was sound and safe. Dr. Mina's mother wasn't back. Neither was Roya. When we whispered, the hooded repentant kept hushing us. Finally she raised her voice and said, "If you keep talking, I'll call Sister Soghra to take care of you!"

We kept quiet.

23

There were two blackouts. The first one was the prison blackout and it meant that we had to sleep. But no one took this seriously. If we didn't have a Raven, we kept talking until late. But the city blackout was the serious one. After that we had to sleep. That night there was barely enough room to stretch our legs out. So I squeezed against the cell door and gave my room to Leila. I told her that I'd done this before. I'd rather get some sleep in the morning.

Sitting there, pressing against the iron door, I held the shutter of the tray window open to let the breeze in. The corridor was cool and if I held the shutter up all night the air would circulate. But it was tiring to do this. I let it go and a few minutes later I lifted it up again to get a breath of fresh air. The women were moaning, weeping, and mumbling meaningless words in their dreams. Someone suddenly screamed and sat up. Another woman held her tightly in her arms and calmed her down.

The tray window was small, but I kept looking at it, fantasizing. What if I'd creep out of this window and get a good night's sleep in the cool corridor? Then early in the morning Baba would let me in. He would be bringing the morning tea. Soghra and the other guards were busy in the temporaries' hall, they wouldn't come to check all night. Now I measured the width of my shoulders against the width of the opening. It was the same. My hips were certainly smaller. I had lost a lot of weight in the past few days. I could pass through.

First I stuck my head out. The hall was empty. The yellow bulbs cast a gloomy light. I pushed myself through the opening until my shoulders were in the frame. I wriggled them, pushing further. Now my shoulders were released and I was suddenly sliding, head first, toward the corridor's floor. My body slipped out of the small square window like a baby into the midwife's hands.

The corridor was cool and empty, but anxiety wouldn't let me sleep. I lay on the hard floor, alert, listening to the distant sounds. What if Jamali or Soghra should come? They would hang me upside down. Now I regretted crawling out. That was a childish thing to do. While I was debating whether to get back into the cell or not, I heard footsteps. From the left end of the hall a woman appeared. She had the black veil of the female guards, but didn't wear boots. Her shoes had heels. Although the heels were not high, they made a hollow knocking sound on the cement. The sound echoed in the empty corridor. When she stopped in front of a cell door in the middle of the hall, I saw her profile. She was the same woman with pockmarks and long dagger-shaped eyebrows, the woman who had made me mop the floor while I was bleeding. She fished a long key chain out of her pocket, opened the door, and went inside. I waited for her to come out.

Finally she came out, dragging something out of the cell. If this was a body, it was the body of a small woman or a child. Now, like a magician, she drew something else from under her wide chador. It was a burlap sack. She opened its mouth and stuffed the small figure into the sack. Briskly, she tied the mouth of the sack. Then dragging it behind her on the cement floor, she walked away in the direction she had come from, her heels knocking.

All this time I'd been pressing myself against the wall, hoping to melt into it and disappear. But now I stretched my body and exhaled with relief. This relief lasted only a short time; I panicked again and couldn't make myself lie down and sleep. I sat awkwardly, knees into my chest, dozing off. Several times I woke myself, thinking that I had heard the knocking of the woman's high heels. I felt as if I were naked, sitting in the middle of a dark street, but any moment the lights would expose me and all the people of the world would see me. I had to hide myself, but I didn't know how. There was nothing to hide behind, to sink into, or to climb on. I could try to squeeze myself back into the cell, but now I had this fear that I was going to get stuck in the frame and somebody would arrive.

"Hey what are you doing there?" Someone was talking to me from the tray window of the opposite cell. "If they catch you they'll give you a hard time. Come to our cell."

"But—"

"Tomorrow we'll tell Baba to switch your room. Come, I'll help you squeeze in."

"Is your cell full?"

"No. Just five people. They've taken out most of them. They say there's going to be another 'Cleaning-Up Operation.'"

"Another what?

"Cleaning Up. Drrrrr...," she made the sound of a machine gun.

I stuck my head in their cell and she helped me to pull my shoulders in. My thin waist and narrow hips slipped in easily.

They had a stocking-hooded repentant in their cell, but she

was in a deep sleep, snoring uncomfortably. Feeling hot, the Raven had pulled the stocking up above her eyes. She was on her back, her facial muscles twitching. I kept staring at her until the girl who had let me in shook me, breaking the spell.

"Do you know her?" The girl asked.

"No. I don't think so."

But I knew her. This was Ferial, my sister-in-law. Her small birdlike body was spread flat like a sparrow run over by a car. Her head was tilted to one side; the black stocking was folded above her eyebrows. I looked at her belly. It wasn't big. Then I saw Dr. Mina's Mother curled up in a corner. Roya was sleeping in this cell too, with her horn braids sticking out of her scarf. Her face was covered with patches of red and blue.

The girl who took me in introduced herself as Nahid, a journalist. She showed me the blisters on her soles. She had been whipped in the empty pool the same night that Leila was whipped. She said that very soon there would be enough space in the cells, because they were going to execute those who hadn't cooperated. She said it was true that they removed the girls' virginity. But she wasn't sure how. Maybe they married them to the guards for a few minutes. I asked her about the visitations. She said it was on Friday evening, the night before. I realized that it was Sunday now, and Friday when Mali had come to visit me, I'd been standing blindfolded in a place called the barn.

Like old friends, Nahid and I talked through the night. Although I was ten years younger, I didn't feel our age difference. She said her only desire was to survive and write about the Bathhouse. She said she was writing in her head every day and that made everything easier for her. She had the first chapter of her book ready, all in her head. I told her that my father had been a writer in his youth. Then he quit writing, but kept thinking about it, regretting all his life that he had given it up. Nahid shook her head and sighed. Then we talked about our fears. She said she was a virgin, she feared her eventual rape. I said I feared the pockmarked woman with dagger-shaped eyebrows.

Early morning, when Baba slid the tray in the cell, Nahid called him in and asked him to take me back to my cell. Baba said that in the past seventy-five years working in this prison, this was the first time he had witnessed such a thing. To slide out of the small, narrow, tray window like a fish was unseen and unheard of. He said that I was the thinnest, tiniest little creature he'd ever seen here. Then he grumbled, saying that this was a heavy responsibility for him, but then he shook his fuzzy head and took me out. Nahid and I embraced as if we had been friends for ages and we were not going to see each other again.

When I entered our cell, everyone was shocked. They had thought that the guards had taken me out last night for further interrogation. Leila's eyes were asking if I was all right. I smiled at her. I couldn't talk. Our hooded repentant who assumed that I was being interrogated all night looked at my face carefully to find new bruises.

I sat down next to Dr. Mina and whispered into her ear: "Your mother is in the opposite cell, sleeping soundly."

She held my head in her hands and kissed my cheeks. Then she took her glasses off, dabbed her eyes nervously, and wiped her foggy lenses with her scarf.

24

We were standing in the toilet line when Soghra leashed me and dragged me to the temporary. She left me in Jamali's room on the same chair where I sat for interrogation the first evening. Ali played in a corner with a match box. He ran it on the floor like a truck, and made a low but steady groan in his throat. This was the only sound I'd heard coming out of this child. I watched him and he looked at me from under his eyelids. He recognized me. I smiled and he blinked several times, which made me think that he was trying to smile back. The corner of his lips slightly moved.

Now the door opened and Jamali came in. He had one of his wash-and-wear shirts on, a white one, with yellow rings under the armpits. He was greasier than ever. His face shone.

"Someone wants to see you. I'll leave the room and let you two talk. Hey, Ali, come with me. Let's get out of here and have some lunch."

On the way out he told the guard to let the prisoners visit for ten minutes and then send them to their cells. The guard was Mohsen, the same young lad who acted like movie stars. Mohsen brought my brother in. Hamid was blindfolded. Mohsen sat him on a chair, removed his blindfold, and left the room.

"Ten minutes," he yelled at the door.

We sat for a long moment looking at each other. I decided that I was not going to cry. Later in the cell, maybe, but not here. I sat like a statue, watching my brother. He still had that olive green shirt on—the one I'd bought him for his birthday a few months ago. His face was thin and pale. He had lost a lot of weight. His slanted eyes looked larger. They hadn't shaved his mustache, but they had shaved his curly hair.

"They've beaten you with those silly rulers," he said calmly, staring at my face. "Have you seen this red line?" He ran his finger across my right cheek.

"I haven't seen myself since they brought us here."

"It's exactly a week."

"Is it? I thought it was much longer."

"It seems long. Very long."

Then we kept quiet for a while.

"Listen, Ferial is—"

"I know," I interrupted him. "You don't need to say anything."

"She is pregnant."

"I know."

"They let us talk because I'm on the next list."

"I know," I said and swallowed a big ball. I was not going to cry.

"Tonight or tomorrow."

"Yes."

"They'll let you go. I'm sure. I've told them one million times that you were not involved in anything. They know it, too."

"I know they know it."

"Go to the medical school."

"Okay."

"Take care of Mali."

"I will."

"Ferial is going to stay here. With our baby."

"I know."

"Forgive her."

I didn't know what to say. Who was I to forgive anyone? Maybe he meant that he had forgiven her. We sat for another long moment and looked at each other. Now that his face was thinner, he resembled our mother. He had Mommy's straight nose, her light brown eyes with yellow-green specks in the irises. Hamid's eyebrows were so neatly shaped that one would think that he had trimmed them. His moustache was light brown. Blondish.

"I keep remembering the stars," I said.

"Which stars?"

"Do you remember on the roof? You showed me the stars? When my knees were injured? I was nine or ten."

"Oh. . . "

He started to think, creased his forehead and nodded. But I'm not sure if he remembered.

'You said whenever you had a problem you thought about the vast universe and your problem seemed small to you."

"Ah. . . "

"They made us stand on our legs the other night. Until morning. I was one of the three who didn't collapse. Because of what you said—the stars."

"You're strong."

"Me?"

"Yes. Very."

"I don't think so."

"You are."

We became silent again. Hamid had changed. He used to be very talkative. Full of energy. Something had drained out of him.

"Hamid, you haven't told them anything, have you?"

"About what?"

"About your friends."

"I've told them what they already knew. Dead information."

"Then why—?"

"Because I can't repent. I believe in my ideas. It's a war. You see? A war of ideas. They've won and they have the power. Had we won, we would have done the same thing to them."

"The same?"

"More or less."

"Your time is over. Get up!" Mohsen who was eavesdropping came in. "Stay here," he ordered me, "Sister Soghra will take you."

Before he blindfolded Hamid, we embraced. I put my head between his neck and shoulder and took a deep breath. I wanted to keep something of him in my body. There was nothing else I could take, so I tried to breathe him in.

"Keep your good spirit," Hamid said. "You'll get out soon."

I couldn't utter a word. Not even goodbye.

I didn't talk or eat the rest of the day. I sat with my head resting on my knees in front of the small window where I had scratched the paint off. I sat there waiting to hear the sound of the iron mountain falling. I knew that it could happen any time of the day or night. As the time passed, I became restless; I wanted it to happen soon. I knew that Hamid was calm, but he was very sad too. I didn't want him to suffer.

At dusk Soghra came in, whispered something in Leila's ear and left. Leila changed color, went pale. She sat for a long time, motionless. Finally she found her way through the many sitting women and crawled toward me. She held my hand. Her hand was ice cold.

"Listen. In thirty minutes Soghra is coming to get me. I'm on the list."

I looked at her pale face and her glistening black hair, which was always unveiled, exposed like a flag. My eyes burned. But I swallowed the big lump down.

"My brother will be with you. I talked to him today."

"What does he look like? I'll try to stand next to him."

"He has a green shirt on. Handsome face. You'll recognize him."

"I want to ask you a favor," she said in haste, as if she was leaving any minute now.

"What?"

"If you happen to get out of here, go and see my husband."

"I didn't now you had a husband, Leila."

Now she burst into loud laughter. A happy laughter. Her eyes filled with tears. "What made you think that I was single? I'm thirty-five years old."

"I don't know. I just assumed. I'm sorry. How can I find him?"

"Go to the Central Hospital. Dr. Mehran. Tell him I was fine to the last minute. Happy. Tell him to show you our son."

"And a son too?"

"Aha," she laughed.

"Where is he?"

"With my mother. He's four years old. The sweetest little boy. Do that. See my son for me. Tell my husband that you want to see Kami."

"I will."

"Now I need to get ready. I don't want to look miserable. I need some color on my face. Let's all exercise. Hey, everybody. Aren't you tired of sitting?"

She began to talk in an agitated way, as she had when she first came into our cell. She organized three circles in the middle of the room and joined us. She counted the numbers and gave instructions to the women in each circle to turn to the right or left. The three circles turned in different directions while we hopped up and down. Now, like the last time, we sang "The weather is pleasant, the flowers are ... blooming ... the sun is rising ... the spring is coming, the spring is coming!

When Leila left, she was flushed. She embraced all of us, the ones she knew and the ones she didn't know. Soghra gave her a large black scarf to wear; she threw it away. At the last moment Robab rushed toward Leila, dropping herself into her arms, sobbing. She held on to her and didn't let her go. I pulled Robab back, trying to calm her down. She kept screaming and talking incoherently. Mrs. Moradi took her to a corner to calm her down. I looked at Leila for the last time, standing in the frame of the door, smiling. She held up two fingers, then Soghra tightened her leash and pulled her out.

The new inmates thought that Leila was a revolutionary leader, an important activist. They talked about her the rest of the evening. Her raised fingers, her smile, the way she threw the scarf away—all that and more. They added to the story, they exaggerated the scene, and before the blackout, when the iron mountain finally collapsed, in the inmates' hearts and minds, in their muffled whispers and broken conversations, Leila was a hero.

25

I stayed up all night, keeping the door of the tray window open to breathe. I didn't think about Hamid and Leila. I was empty. I felt relaxed in a strange way I hadn't experienced before. I felt physically light, almost weightless. My heartbeats were even and calm and I didn't feel any pain in my body. I took an immense pleasure from the breeze blowing through the tray window, brushing my face. The night was so quiet that although I was not sitting next to the window, I could hear the remote sounds of the outside. First there was the usual laughter and uproar of children, but after a short while the children's voice died out and the sound of the crickets and one solitary toad became distinct. The crickets became silent too, but the toad sang monotonously until morning, as if sitting behind the thick wall of the cell, calling me out. What if this toad was a prince who had come to my rescue? I laughed at myself. This sounded more like the person I used to be—the girl who entered the Bathhouse last week. Who was I now?

In the middle of the night I woke up because an instrument played in my head. It was a cello, but its sound was much deeper. Maybe it was a contrabass, or an instrument that didn't exist in reality. This low-pitched string instrument played a strange and sorrowful tune inside me. Half asleep, I sat and whispered, "Celestial music! It must be for me. They're sending this down for me..." I stayed awake for a long time and the music remained in my head. It repeated the same tune on and on. Deep and remote, dark and grave, it gave out all the sorrows of the world. I didn't move for fear of the music leaving me. Then I fell asleep.

26

After breakfast, when Baba was taking the trays out, Sister Soghra and Brother Jamali came to get Dr. Mina.

"Here, take your clothes, Madame. You're released. Your husband and son are waiting at the gate."

Dr. Mina got to her feet. Her knees buckled; someone held her up. In one week she had turned into a sack of bones. She wasn't more than forty years old, but her gray hair showed more white than black.

"But my mother?"

"I said you are released," Jamali repeated impatiently.

"I won't leave without my mother. Where is she?"

"She is fine. She'll join you later. Hurry up. Your husband and son have been waiting since early morning."

"I won't leave her here," she wept into her palms.

"She's crazy," Jamali told Soghra. "I don't have time to waste here. People are waiting in my office. If she really doesn't want to leave, let me know." He left.

Mrs. Moradi and several older women circled Dr. Mina, urging her to change and leave.

"Get out of here so that you can do something for your mother," Mrs. Moradi said.

"What can you do here, huh?" Another woman asked.

"Here, give us the clothes, Sister. She'll change." The women grabbed Dr. Mina's clothes from Soghra.

"I'll be back in five minutes. Be ready," Soghra said.

"But she is here. My mother is here in one of these rooms," Dr. Mina said. She sounded delirious. Confused.

My heart banged against my chest. What if she'd tell Soghra that I had seen her mother? She was beside herself and wouldn't realize that she was endangering me.

"Who told you that your mother was here? Huh?"

Dr. Mina didn't say anything.

"Did you see her with your own eyes? She is in the clinic. Didn't you insist that she needed to see a doctor? Yes or no? Answer me!"

"Yes."

"Well, she is in the clinic. She'll be released after recovery. Now do you want to go home or not?"

"She's ready, Sister. Don't leave!" a woman said. "She's coming," another woman, who was putting Mina's dress on her, said. The women all talked at the same time and interrupted each other.

"Where are her shoes now?"

"Let her go with the slippers."

"She can't take the prison's property out," Soghra raised her voice.

"Stop crying now. You're going out. You'll see your son."

"How old is your son?"

"Fifteen."

"Hurry up, your young man is waiting."

"To hell with the shoes, let her go barefoot. Just let her go!"

Someone said.

"What if—" Dr. Mina's face was now blank as a stone statue and wet with tears. As the women dressed her, she swayed like a willow in the wind. She was on the verge of collapsing. "What if she's dead?"

"She is not dead. She is not. Go!" The women pushed her out of the cell.

Soghra slammed the door, but we heard her hollering in the hallway: "—and you call yourself a doctor, too? What kind of a doctor are you anyway, crying like a baby? Pull yourself together and act like a grown-up!"

After this commotion it took us a while to calm down. Some women believed that Dr. Mina's mother was dead and that was why they were releasing her in such haste. They didn't want her to find out. Some said she was in the clinic. They couldn't release her with a bad back; it would reveal torture. I kept quiet, now doubting that the woman I saw in the cell opposite was Mina's mother.

At lunch, Baba brought the news that Dr. Mina had finally left the Bathhouse.

"The husband looked exactly like the wife," Baba said, "serious looking, thick lenses, gray hair. But their son was a tall young man with a thin mustache above his lips. He stood there as stiff as he could, neck stretched up like a rooster. But when his mother stepped out in the street, small as a bird and barefoot, the boy broke." Baba sighed and shook his head. "He became a baby again. . . . Well, girls, this was the street scene for today, let's see what will happen tomorrow." He murmured this to himself and left the cell.

From our old group, only Mrs. Moradi, Robab and I were left. In Leila's absence, Robab had started to act out again. She complained about the machine being broken, and the baby growing bigger every minute. At dusk, before dinner, Robab began to have her labor. She spread her hefty body on the floor, opened her legs wide apart, screaming. She punched her belly, which was really fat, and cursed the authorities:

"What kind of prison is this if they don't have a midwife! Send me a midwife! No, not a midwife, she wouldn't know how to take the machine out. A doctor must open my belly. Ay! Ay! It hurts. . . . Help!"

The more the women tried to keep her quiet, the more Robab hollered. Finally Soghra and two hooded repentants came in and dragged her out.

"Solitary! That's where you belong!" Soghra said angrily.

"No, please! I'll die there. The baby will die!"

"Which baby, huh? You dirty bitch!" Soghra slapped her right and left and Robab instantly became quiet as if all she needed was a couple of slaps.

While the repentants were putting handcuffs on Robab and tying a leash on her neck, she turned and looked at us pleadingly, as if we had the power to do something for her. Her dark, crookedly cut hair had grown longer at the roots and it was half black and half reddish-blond, curling above her ears like a clown's wig. She left with her baby and the machine in her belly, and I never found out who she was, or who she had been before the Bathhouse.

The same day they took Mrs. Moradi out and I was left alone

with inmates I hadn't had the spirit to get close to. They were from all age groups—a few older women, a few middle-aged, and young girls too, some very young, with school uniforms. The school girls still had long hair and when a hooded repentant was not sitting in our room, they removed their scarves, combed their hair with their finger tips, and made them into braids or buns behind their necks. Meanwhile they talked about outside, the massive arrests in the streets, houses, schools, and offices. I overheard one woman saying that she was a math teacher, teaching summer classes, when the guards invaded the school and arrested her. They blindfolded her in front of her students. The students screamed, cried, and called her name. They chased the black van to get her back. The woman said that their little voices were all she remembered from outside—the wailing and screaing of twenty-five children

27

One day all the long-braided girls became bald. They shaved our hair. Some of the girls wept quietly. I remembered the day they cut Roya's braids and the way she reacted. I was grateful that she was not here today. The older ladies looked strange with their bald heads. I'd never seen an old woman without hair. But no one laughed. We looked ridiculous but it was horrible, too. Some of the women had bumpy heads, not quite round, strangely shaped. I realized that when we have hair we think our heads are round, but this is not true. There was a woman the back of whose head was flat like a board. We watched each other out of the corners of our eyes, trying not to stare, not to embarrass anyone. The mood was not like the day we took a shower and laughed at our funny appearances. Losing our hair was worse than nakedness—it was losing face, being exposed. When Soghra and her assistant finished the job, swept the floor, and left with their electric shavers, we all covered our heads with our large scarves and sat quietly. I thought that if Leila were alive she would make everybody exercise now. No one had Leila's spirit. We sat still, listening to the monotonous sound of one girl's weeping under her chador.

I was indifferent to my baldness; I didn't care a bit. Now I slept most of the time. I slept as long as I could. I slept instead of eating and talking with my cell mates. I even missed the Friday shower. I waited for that cello, but it never played in my head again. I thought that I was confused that night and the tune never existed.

Mrs. Moradi didn't return. I kept imagining her sitting on a chair, watching her son hanging from his feet, swaying like a pendulum. This was a recurring image, I saw it in dreams and daydreams: Mrs. Moradi, sitting on a stool, her boy hanging, until she notices blood dripping out of her son's nose and mouth. She screams and tells the guards that she'll tell everything if they'll only put her son back on his feet again. When they bring the boy down, he is dead.

Every night after this dream, I sat up in horror, as if this had really happened. I felt a vague joy too. My brother was dead and they could never force me to watch him hanging from his feet.

I thought about my first cell mates more than my family or my present cell mates, as if that group was my real family and that life was my real life. For hours and hours I remembered the night in the barn, the ones who collapsed and the ones who stood until morning. I remembered Leila, her shiny hair, her smile, her raised fingers, her last words to me. Then I thought about the strange and sudden release of Dr. Mina. Where was she now? Could she ever be happy with her family, losing her mother here? I saw her mother in the other cell, didn't I? That small round body with the slightly hunched back, curled on the floor; she was moaning. But what if she died after I saw her? Hadn't I seen the pock-marked woman, the woman with long eyebrows, pulling sacks out of the cells? I repeated Robab's name in my delirium. Robab—crazy from the beginning to the end. I imagined her in a dark, solitary confinement, sitting with her legs apart, talking to herself, punching her fat belly, screaming with real pain.

Gradually I lost track of time. Now my cell mates knew me as someone who didn't talk. A few of them understood, but many didn't. The first group were kind to me, woke me up for food, reminded me of the toilet and shower times. They knew that I'd been here for a long time; I had seen a lot. Those who didn't like me considered me unsociable, weird. They expected me to take part in their group activities. Now they had teams for cleaning the cell, for dividing the food, for exercising, modeled on Leila's circles. They had elected a spokesperson in case someone came to investigate. I didn't take part in any of these activities. I either slept or pretended to sleep.

At times I tried to remember good memories of my past life. But I couldn't recall anything. I decided that in spite of having lived a comfortable life, I'd always been unhappy. I decided that my parents had neglected me, having brought me into this world when they were not young anymore and giving me to my sister to raise. I resented my dead father and mother. I didn't feel that I had missed Mali, either. I didn't like her. I decided that she was a cold woman, a victim of our strange parents, who imposed strict rules on me to satisfy her sense of power. I decided that my life, especially the last two years after our parents' death had not been much better than prison life. Mali never allowed me to take part in the many activities that gave meaning to young people's lives after the revolution. She didn't even allow me to go on the roof with the thousands of other people to watch the moon.

I blamed my dead brother, too. I blamed him for immersing himself in his political life and neglecting me. Couldn't he have taken me out of that house? Couldn't I have become an activist if

he had taken me more seriously? Now that I was in prison anyway, what difference did it make?

I felt worthless, ashamed of being in the Bathhouse only for
writing stupid entries in my journals. I was no one, nothing, and
I was being punished for my stupidity. I blamed myself for taking
Zohre's baby out and worsening my situation. I blamed my family for raising me as a worthless person. Lying down in the corner
of the cell, pretending to be asleep, I felt rage and self-hatred. I
fantasized death. But even my fantasies were cowardly. No poi-
son, no dagger, no bashing my head on the toilet bowl (there were
rumors that a male prisoner had done this), just a desire to van-
ish. I wished that someone, something, would erase me here and
now from this useless life. But I couldn't raise a finger against
myself.

One day there was an uproar in the corridor. All of us rushed
to the tray window to look out. We heard the hysterical screams
of several women beyond our door—a heartbreaking wailing that
lasted for a long time. There was no way to know what had happened. At dinner, instead of sliding the trays in, Baba came and
sat with us. He had a story to tell. When Baba had a juicy prison
scene, he couldn't keep it for himself; he had to share it. His life
consisted of these stories. He couldn't be the one-man audience of
a show; he had to make others see what he'd seen. He was grim
this time. His hump looked bigger. His voice shook. He said that
a girl by the name of Nahid, a journalist, who was in the opposite
cell, hanged herself from the shower. She was on the next death
list. She had told her friends that she was not afraid of death, she
feared the rape.

28

We had entered a period of moonless nights. I lay down next to my small window every night, watching the courtyard's brick floor. There was no reflection of the moon. First I tried to count the number of dark nights, then I gave up. They were many. No one passed through the yard at night, or if they did, it was too dark to see anything. I heard the distant uproar of children, the screams of joy and the laughter. I didn't know where they came from. This uproar always died out before the city blackout. Then the crickets and toads began.

Again I dreamed (or dreamed while I was awake; I could not tell the difference anymore) of my father. An image came to me that belonged to my remote past. We had a jasmine bush in the yard, Papa's favorite. Star jasmine, with tiny white flowers blossoming every dawn. The scent of these small blossoms was so strong that even a tiny one perfumed the house. Papa used to wake up at dawn and fill a dish with jasmine blossoms. He put the blossoms on the dining table before going to work. I was the second person who woke up each morning in our house. When I came downstairs to have breakfast, the room was scented. I picked up a couple of blossoms and put them in my shirt pocket. The smell of the star jasmines stayed with me all day.

Now I lay on the floor of the cell, dreaming, or having a delusion, of my father holding the dish of blossoms under my nose, smiling at me. I told him, "Papa, did you know that I was so much like you? Is that why you avoided me?"

29

Women kept entering the cell and leaving. I was the permanent one. Twice more I heard the fall of the iron mountain behind the wall. A women's appearance and disappearance became faster than ever; at least, it seemed faster to me. Before I'd get used to her face, she'd disappear and the mountain would collapse.

One day I opened my eyes and the cell was empty. Baba brought tea and a piece of bread for me and lingered to talk.

"Do you want to hear a street scene, girl?"

"No," I said. I was short tempered, didn't want to talk to anyone, nor hear anything.

"You've been here longer than everybody I know. Maybe they've forgotten you. Tell Soghra that you want to talk to Jamali; I'm telling you, girl, they must have forgotten you."

"So much the better," I said.

"Well, well, well. This is not a good spirit. Let me tell you a story about a prisoner who had a better spirit than you." He sat down cross-legged as if he were my grandfather and this was our home where we were having tea together. "Have a sip of your tea now. I brewed it myself. I knew that you were alone here. I made you a special tea." He was lying, of course, but it pleased me.

"This story goes back to the time of the old king when my father was a janitor here and I was a little boy helping him out. Have you seen that tiny Ali? Jamali's son? I was that age and carried the trays to the cells, helping my father out. He paid me a black coin or two to buy myself sugar candies every day. Anyway, it was either in this same room that we're sitting now or in the next one, that a tall handsome doctor was locked up. He was fresh from foreign lands—I don't know which one exactly, France, Germany, or, where. But that's how he had become a doctor. Doctor of what? I don't have any idea. I don't think he was a physician, though. Anyway, his friends called him doctor all the time. He and fifty-two prisoners filled the cells of this hallway, all members of one group. They had come from abroad to change the government, which was a monarchy at that time. They wanted a socialist government here. Lenin was still alive in Russia and the Bolsheviks were very popular. Now you can figure out how old I am, girl. Very old. I was seven years old when Lenin was the leader in Russia.

"In any case, the old king had ordered his guards to torture the members of this group and then kill them. They didn't have repentants at that time. There wasn't a second chance for people. You rise against the monarchy? You get killed. Period. If you think about it, these people are more charitable, they give the prisoners a chance to repent and cooperate and stay alive. Agree?"

I kept quiet and just looked at his yellow face. Perhaps because he stayed indoors all the time, his face was jaundiced and full of strange blue patches, as if he had some kind of skin disease. His eyes were green and playful, much younger than he said he was. He had a prickly beard and mustache and only a few long, yellow teeth. Maybe Jamali had sent him to make me repent. But repent of what?

"To make a long story short," he went on, "this doctor one

night broke that little window and went out of the cell. The windows weren't barred from outside then. It was a moonless night, he ran in the courtyard, but he couldn't find the gate. You know that this building is circular, but at that time it wasn't just one circle; it was made of three circles, one inside the other, like a maze. The doctor ran and ran, but he was running in a circle around the prison. There was no gate. He didn't know that he must find the narrow opening to the second circle and another narrow opening to the last circle and there the gate was. All the time the guards, sitting on the roof, drinking vodka, were watching him and laughing. It was very easy to guard this building back then; they didn't need watch dogs or armed soldiers in the courtyards. Every night the guards just sat on the roof, enjoyed the cool breeze, and got drunk."

"I didn't know about the circles."

"It's not made of three circles anymore. I'm talking about seventy-five years ago. At the time of the young king, when I started my job, for some reason, they removed the first and the second walls and only the inner circle, which is this courtyard and the building in the middle, stayed."

We sat in silence for a minute, then Baba stood up to leave. "But have I ever told you that this building was a real bathhouse once?"

"I've heard that."

"That was before my father, before the old king. It was at the time of the old dynasty. More than one hundred years ago. This area was the center of the capital and this was the best bathhouse. I always imagine that the pool is full of fresh water, the chambers around the pool are full of men, dressing and undressing, and there are sounds of splash and gurgle and the bare hands of the bath keepers massaging the wet skins. What a time. . . . Have you ever been to a public bath? No, you're too young to know what a public bath is."

"I know what it is, but I've never been to one. There are none left."

"True. None left. Well, keep your spirit up, girl. Don't sleep too much!"

"Hey, Baba," I called him before he closed the door. "What happened to the doctor? The one who was lost in the maze?"

"I won't tell you all the things that they did to him. I'll just tell you his end. They injected air into his vein. There was an uprising out there. They couldn't shoot him from fear of the people, his followers. People loved him, you know. So they pretended that he died of natural causes."

"I'd never heard about him before."

"I'm sure the kids who go to the Wall of the Almighty every day have heard about him. He is famous."

Baba left and I heard the key turning in the keyhole.

For a while I sat motionless, not thinking about the doctor in the maze, but about Baba and his long life here. Why did he tell me the story of an unsuccessful escape? Didn't he say he wanted to cheer me up, lift my spirits? Or were all of Baba's stories morbid like this one?

The cell remained empty until lunchtime, then the door opened and Soghra pushed someone in. It was Roya, the high school girl of the first group, the girl who didn't want to lose her long braids and ended up with two short horns behind her ears, the girl who kept washing herself under the dry shower. She sat motionless, as if she didn't know me.

"Roya! Don't you remember me?"

She didn't answer. Half of her face was bruised black and blue. She had this black scarf on, tied tightly under her chin; I couldn't see her hair. She sat and stared at the opposite wall. I kept calling her, but then I gave up. I thought that she must have gone out of her mind; otherwise she would say something to me. With Roya mute, someone from my former life, the only life I'd lived in my entire life, I felt even lonelier. She was one particle of my past proving that I had lived it. Proving that Mrs. Moradi, Dr. Mina, Robab, and Leila, were real and not figments of my imagination. We sat until evening and Roya didn't say a word. Once I asked her if she remembered Robab and her baby and the machine. She didn't react. I asked her if she remembered Leila and for the first time she blinked. I knew that they were very close, Roya always slept next to Leila, laying her head on Leila's shoulder. I sat in front of Roya, looked into her eyes, and repeated Leila's name.

"I'm sure you remember Leila. Tell me about her. Talk to me."

It was dusk when she burst into tears. I held her in my arms, patted her back, and kept telling her, "Cry Roya! Cry, cry, cry—"

30

Roya became attached to me like a baby. She lay her head on my shoulder every night and didn't let me sleep. I was the only one she knew. The only one who knew Leila. For a couple of days we were alone in the cell, but Roya was mute. I talked to her about myself, the school I went to, the teachers, and told her little stories to entertain her. She listened but I wasn't sure if she understood a word. Her face was expressionless, as if she were listening attentively to a language she didn't know.

On the third day, they suddenly opened the iron door and prodded a dozen women in. The guards, Soghra, and the others were armed; they had machine guns in their hands, aimed at these women. They cursed them and shoved them in with the muzzles of their guns. The girls were all blindfolded. They fell, rolling over each other. Roya squeezed herself to me; she was ready to cry like a baby witnessing other children's punishment.

After Soghra and the guards locked the door, the women removed their blindfolds. They were all young, between twenty and thirty. Not one middle-aged or in her teens. Before long, they began to clean the cell. They all worked together with discipline, rubbing and scrubbing the floor, spreading the prison chadors on the floor like carpet. Then they sat in a circle and introduced themselves to us. They were all together—members of one organization. I talked for Roya. I said that she wouldn't speak. Couldn't.

They asked me how long had I been here and how the conditions were—was it true that they had executed hundreds of prisoners without a real trial? I said it was true and told them about the sound of the iron mountain collapsing every few days. I told them about my cell mates, how one by one they disappeared. Roya and I were left. Then they asked me if it was okay for me to tell them who I was and what I'd done. I told them that I was nobody. Graduated from high school a few months ago and was getting ready to go to college. I wasn't political. I didn't mention my brother and his wife. They said so it was true that they'd bring ordinary people here, mixing them with the politicals. I told them it was true.

Now they sang a song together. With much emotion and intensity and in unison, as if they'd sung it many times before. They exercised and then sat for a long meeting. They told me that they were members of an armed guerilla group; they were arrested together because someone who was arrested earlier had betrayed them and showed their team house to the guards. Most of the things they discussed in their meeting were beyond my understanding. They talked in a political language with special terms. I'd heard Hamid and Ferial talking like this before: "... the severe protracted economic crisis ... the ability of the clerical leadership to consolidate its power ... the situation of the proletariat and the peasants..." and so on. They talked and talked and analyzed the situation as if they were going to spend one night in jail and return to their guerilla fighting the next day. Roya and I sat in a corner, watching them as if this were a movie or these girls were from another planet.

31

The next morning, early, before toilet and breakfast, they took us out to the courtyard, where the empty pool was, where once the rituals of flogging had happened, where Ferial saw the Leader on the moon and repented in public. We stood around the pool and I noticed that the ground was covered with pebbles and stones. This courtyard had a brick floor; obviously they had brought stones and covered the brick floor. No one knew what was going on. Armed guards were standing around, aiming at us. They brought more and more inmates out, all women, from the temporary and permanent cells. We were the first group, so they stood us right by the pool. Then the pock-marked woman with long eyebrows—I'd never learned her name—dragged a girl by a leash and pushed her into the empty pool. Soghra dragged another girl and did the same thing with her. They dumped them like garbage bags in the ditch. Now Brother Jamali appeared from one of the chambers around the pool and raised his voice.

"We're going to stone these whores today. If you don't throw stones, you'll end up down here yourselves. Understood?"

"But why?" someone, a voice from my left side, asked innocently.

"Who said 'why'? Huh? There must be a reason, or we would not spend our time stoning people. We're not crazy and we have other things to do. It shames me to tell you why. I can't talk about it. Sister, can you find the right words to explain this punishment?" he asked the pock-marked woman.

"I'll try, Brother Jamali," she said in her husky voice. "These dirty bitches are sick. You know what I mean? The repentant sister who sleeps in their cell woke up last night to have a sip of water and she saw them in each other's arms. Busy. You get me?"

"Enough now!" Jamali said. "Now they know. Pick a stone and teach them a lesson. If you don't cooperate, it means that you approve their act."

Jamali, the pock-mocked woman, Soghra, and other male and female guards and repentants whose number had grown each lifted a stone and threw it. The inmates were hesitant. Some girls cried.

"Do you all want to go down in the pool? Huh? Pick up a stone, It's an order!"

Some women picked a very small pebble and threw. The first ones were slow and hesitant, then the rhythm became faster. There was a shower of stones on the girls in the empty pool. They were on all fours like animals, trying to protect themselves with their arms curved over their heads. A sharp thing pushed against my belly. It was a gun.

"Pick one up, bitch! Hurry up, or you'll go down, too." This was a hooded repentant. Those repentants who were trustworthy could carry guns.

I picked up a pebble and threw it in the pool. Then I picked up more. None hit them. I just kept doing it so that the Raven would leave me alone. Many girls didn't cooperate. The guards pushed them in the pool and others hit them. Now there were several women in the pool and I could see the blood. I tried not to look inside the pool, at the bloody heads and the bruised bodies. How long was this to go on? Why wouldn't they stop? They kept throwing. I saw more blood and more girls being prodded inside the pool. I threw and threw, not controlling my aim anymore, not being careful to avoid hurting anyone. I threw the stones because this hooded repentant, this armed Raven was pressing the muzzle of her gun to my belly and if I'd stop picking up stones and throwing at the girls, she'd either push me in the bloody pool or shoot me. I threw more, small and big, round or sharp. I threw until someone next to me screamed with horror. The scream came from the bottom of her lungs and pierced my eardrums. She shrieked. She ripped her scarf off, baring her bald head; she tore her black uniform open, she undressed, shrieked again, and then jumped in the pool of dust and blood to be stoned with everyone else.

This was Roya. I called her in the chaos of dust, screams, and gunshots. I called her but she didn't hear me. She was half-naked, rolling among the bloody women. Now embracing them, now kissing them, licking their bloody heads, crying, crying for them and with them until they shot so many bullets in the air that the whole world became quiet. Then it was so silent that I could hear a single mockingbird, crying somewhere in a tree outside the Bathhouse. The bird was trying to imitate human sound.

32

Nothing was unbearable after the stoning. Nothing was painful or scary. How simple and easy was our life in the Bathhouse. How calm was everyone. How well we slept, how well we ate. Roya was missing for a whole day, then she returned to our cell, her body black and blue. Her bald head was bandaged and she was sedated, absent. The guerilla fighters went for interrogation and came back, one by one, bruised or bandaged, but none of them moaned or cried. That first meeting was their last meeting, though; a Raven resided in our cell, permanently.

I was hoping that Roya wouldn't come back and when she did I became worried. I didn't want her close to me. She would hang on me, stick to my skin like a leech. I didn't want her to sleep next to me, resting her head on my shoulder. I didn't want the Raven to see us together. When she came I tried to keep my distance, but Roya followed me around the room, quietly, ghost-like. Wherever I sat, she sat next to me, making herself into a ball close to my belly. I sat up every night in case the Raven woke up and checked on us. I didn't have peace anymore, that letting go, that quiet time with myself. Roya became my torment. Sleeping for a short time in the afternoon, I dreamed about us, Roya and I, rolling naked in the pool of dirt and blood, the guards and inmates stoning us. I woke up in horror, unable to sleep any more.

So when, after a few days, they took us to the barn again, I felt relieved. Jamali, Soghra, and the man with the military uniform—Brother Hosseini—came and blindfolded us. Maybe that was when I should've called Jamali's attention to myself, reminding him who I was. Maybe I should've said, "Brother Jamali, remember me? I'm that little brat with those stupid journals. I'm not an armed guerilla or anything like that. Why should I be punished with them?" But I didn't say a word. My tongue felt heavy as a wet brick and my voice didn't come out. The cell was crowded and in our identical black uniforms we all looked alike. I was one of the guerilla fighters now and they took us in Brother Hosseini's van.

Jamali said, "I'll let you all rot in the boxes." I didn't understand what he meant. What boxes? Where? But when they pulled us out of the van and shoved us inside cardboard cartons, I realized what he meant. They made us each sit in a box, which had barely enough space for one person; the front was open. We sat all day with our blindfolds on and at first it wasn't that bad—only sitting in the dark, that's all. But at night they opened the blindfolds and let us eat. I tried to find something to look at, but there was nothing, except a dry lot in front of us. The sky was cloudy, no stars or moon were visible.

I wasn't sure if this was the same location where I once stood until morning. The first time, I'd heard toads and toads were always where trees were. But now I just saw an empty lot with no surrounding walls. Of course, I couldn't bend forward to look around; maybe I'd be able to see trees if I could. I didn't know if this was part of the Bathhouse. The van had driven us a short time, as if taking us from one part of camp to another. The first trip had been short, too.

At night, my body began to ache. Not only were my legs asleep, millions of sharp needles piercing them, but my back, neck, shoulders, and head hurt. I wanted to stretch my legs, but I couldn't. They'd told us that if we moved they'd shoot us. The worst thing was not being able to see each other. I knew that our boxes were all in one row, seventeen boxes. Fifteen guerilla fighters, Roya, and I.

Once I heard a male guard shouting at someone, cursing and insulting her: "If you move your fucking legs one more time, I'll shoot you! Sit straight."

"I need to use the bathroom," the girl said.

"Use it!" A woman said. "This is your home, go to the toilet!" The guards laughed.

"I'm serious, I need to—"

"I'm serious too. Shut up!"

It was quiet for a long time, then I heard someone weeping. I wasn't sure if it was the woman who wanted to use the bathroom or someone else. I hadn't used the bathroom, either. No one had. They took us early in the morning before the toilet time. I decided not to make this into a big issue. If I needed to empty myself, I would. I didn't want to develop a kidney or bladder disease like I'd heard some women had.

A while later my toad sang in the dark and made me smile. I breathed deeply and listened to him. Then suddenly the clouds became luminous as if a torch were flaming underneath them. The clouds moved rapidly and became thinner in some parts, thicker in others. The thin clouds veiled the iridescent moon like transparent silk. Oh, it's not bad at all, I thought, if only I could stretch my legs. Just once and for a few minutes. This sky can amuse me forever and my toad is singing.

But the thick, black clouds won, the torch died, and darkness grew. The toad didn't sing anymore and I heard rain drops on the cardboard roof of my box. It rained and the guards murmured something to each other and came and went, asking Brother Hosseini what to do next—keep us out in the rain or not. I knew that the girls were hoping that Hosseini would cancel the punishment and send us back to our cell. But we sat in the boxes and it rained on us. The cardboard boxes became wet and soggy and the rain dripped on us. Water ran under the boxes and in a short while we were all soaking wet.

Now I was biting my lips. The pain in my legs was intolerable. They wouldn't really shoot me, would they? I tried to stretch my right leg, but I couldn't. I was paralyzed. I tried more, again I couldn't. Either my limbs were not working anymore, or I wasn't trying hard enough to move my legs from the fear of being shot.

The rain stopped just as the cardboard boxes were beginning to collapse. Thin clouds showed again and I saw the moon moving behind them. When the moon became more visible, I saw that it was round, but not quite round. It was like a chipped porcelain saucer. Now the whole disc came out, luminous but shadowed. This was the silhouette of a sea, the sea of tranquility. I remembered Leila saying, "This shadow is a sea ... a sea.... "

I heard my neighbor sighing; I sighed the way she sighed and this way we talked to each other. The moon moved right in front of us and now someone screamed, "I can see it! I can see it!"

"Shut up!" a guard shouted.

"I can see the image of the Great Leader. It's the Holy Leader!"

The guards and repentants all talked at once and I sensed chaos. The girl kept screaming, "Believe me. It's Him. It's his Holy Image!"

Then I heard Brother Hosseini's voice ordering the guards to take the girl to his office. She kept swearing and crying. This was Roya. After weeks of silence she was talking.

For a while after they took Roya to the office, the guards and repentants looked at the moon and debated. Some said the girl lied to get out of the box, the image appeared only on the full moon, but a few others said they saw the image too, the girl didn't lie, she observed it and she must be blessed and forgiven.

This conversation ended soon because of the problem that I created. I felt dizzy and weak. I hadn't slept well since the stoning incident and hadn't eaten for twenty-four hours. I swayed first, then fell forward a few times and finally fell onto my right side. I knocked over my neighbor's box, she knocked over her neighbor's, and all the boxes collapsed like a house of cards. The guards started to beat us with the butt of their machine guns. We lay in puddles of rainwater and the blows were coming at us from everywhere. Now Brother Hosseini came and stopped them. He ordered them to make us sit up again, with or without the boxes. He said that Jamali's order was to make us sit for a week and this was only the end of the first day.

After that I lost track of time. I remember they brought us food. I remember rejecting the food and just drinking water. I remember peeing on myself. I remember the foul odor rising from other boxes. I remember sobs, crazy, delirious murmurs, girls talking to themselves. I remember slaps and kicks, sudden hysterical outbursts, "Don't beat me! Don't!"

The moon kept growing fuller; no one could watch it anymore. Shortly they brought us new boxes. These were TV cartons. In the dim light of the night I recognized pictures of TV sets on them. I don't remember what exactly happened after the new boxes. The whole thing is foggy and confused: Eating, drinking, emptying, dozing off while sitting. Sitting. Collapsing. Being beaten. Day. Night. Blindfold at daytime, clouds and moon at night. The moon rounder, bigger, yellower.

I didn't hear Roya's voice anymore. I felt a vague joy, thinking that she had repented and was lying down in a clean, dry cell now. Wishing I could do the same, I began to consider the possibility. But how could I pretend? I wasn't a good actor. At school performances I was never picked for major roles; I was always in the crowd, feeling awkward and self-conscious, hiding myself behind the other students. How could I scream now, pretending that I was seeing a picture on the moon? But what if Roya wasn't acting, what if she believed that she saw the picture? I didn't believe in anything now. Absolutely nothing. Even that old, kind, fatherly god, that patient and generous old man that I had created for myself to ask him silly things, was long dead. He died the first day in the Bathhouse when I heard the iron mountain falling. The old man vanished a long time before I stoned other inmates to save my life.

"The moon is a piece of rock, separated from the earth, rotating around the earth, rotating around the earth, rotating around the earth—" I whispered to myself in my dark box. "The silhouette on the moon is a sea, the sea of tranquility, tranquility, tranquility—" How could I say that it was the picture of a man? And why would I repent? Who was I to repent? Karl Marx? Che Guevara? Rosa Luxemburg? So I just sat and sat and sat and sat and the moon became rounder and rounder, until one day they lifted us up with all our discharges sticking to us and dumped us like sacks of rotten potatoes into Brother Hosseini's black van.

33

We passed out in the cell, half-conscious. Our odor turned our stomachs. Someone vomited. We smelled of the sewer—old water, sweat, and excrement. No one moved to clean herself, to exercise, to hold a meeting.

The same day or the next, they dragged us out and lined us up in the hallway. We were sixteen, members of a famous armed guerilla group. When they took us through the corridor, many heads watched us from the tray-windows. I saw some raised fingers—V signs. Some of the girls, regaining their composure, raised their fists or held a V up. My steps were weak at first, hesitant, but then became stronger as I walked with the group. I stamped my bare feet on the cement as if I had military boots on. I straightened my stooped back, raised my head, and smiled. I knew that many eyes were watching me, admiring me. I didn't know where they were taking us, but I could sense that I'd never go back to that cell, at the end of the permanents' hall again.

They took us to the shower area and let us wash ourselves. We washed in haste for fear of the warm water stopping. Soghra yelled from outside, "take your time, you have twenty minutes shower time." This was unheard of. Five or ten minutes had become twenty. Maybe they wanted to take us to court. I used plenty of that bad smelling soap on myself. Now it was better than French perfumes. I rubbed my bald head that had sprouted rough prickly hair. We washed, dried, put clean black uniforms and chadors on and stood in a single file. Some of the girls had regained their liveliness, as if they had not sat in cardboard boxes for a week. I heard them talking, laughing. Soghra ignored them, didn't yell.

They took us to the courtyard. It was cloudy and I couldn't tell what time of the day it was. They took us inside the pool and ordered us to lie down on our backs. We were hesitant. We were so clean after all. But we did. I looked around. I didn't see any male guard. I didn't see Brother Jamali. But suddenly more than a dozen Ravens with black stockings on their heads and faces ran toward the pool and jumped in. Each Raven approached one of us, sitting next to us. Soghra and other female guards stood around the pool, aiming their machine guns at the Ravens and at us. The Raven who was sitting next to me pulled my skirt up and bared my right leg. Then she fished in her pocket and took a shaving razor and a big black marker out. She shaved a round spot on my calf, then wrote on me. The way I was lying down I couldn't read the words. Now she asked my name. First name and last. I told her. She wrote them on me. When she was asking my name I noticed that her voice shook. This was a familiar voice.

"Zohre?" I whispered.

"Sh... sh... shut up!" she said. The first day when we met in the interrogation room she had told me to shut up too.

"Zohre..." I whispered again. "What are they going to do with us?"

"It's good for you... good... I envy you... I wish I were you...," she whispered.

"Where is the baby... Rosa...?"

"Sh... sh...." she repeated. "She is not Rosa anymore. They changed her name."

Then she finished writing on me and helped me to rise. When she was pulling me up to stand in line with the others, she squeezed my hand. I wished I could see her green eyes, the way I saw them one day while she was feeding her baby. How beautiful she was.

We stood in a single file inside the empty pool, the sixteen of us, facing the prison. Soghra stepped forward. She had a piece of paper in her hand—a list. She called some of the girls out. I didn't have the slightest idea why she was pulling some of us out. The ones who left the pool were led by a guard to one of the chambers. Soghra watched us carefully. We were seven in the line now. She studied us one by one, as if matching the face with the name in her list. Now she stopped at me and motioned with her finger for me to leave the line and go to her. I climbed up.

"I can't see your name here."

I didn't say anything.

Then she lowered her voice and whispered into my ear, "Are you a virgin?"

I nodded.

"Go to that room, then. Follow that line."

I hesitated for a short moment, staring at the patch of coarse hair on Soghra's left cheek. I kept standing there. My tongue became a wet brick again. I could have explained why my name was not on the list, but I didn't. I didn't have vocal cords.

"Follow them, I said," Soghra said, but not angrily.

I followed the line going toward one of the chambers by the pool.

The room was small and the door was narrow. We had to wait for each inmate to climb one tall stone step, get in the room, and be seated by a guard. Then the next inmate could enter. I saw some metal chairs set up around the room. The inmate who had just entered sat on one of these chairs. I was at the end of the line.

I thought that this room was the last room of my life. And I hoped that the moment would stretch to eternity and I wouldn't go in. I wanted to stay in the courtyard, in the open. The room was the end of everything; it was the other realm. I was ready to be shot right here, not to climb that stone step and sit on a cold metal chair. I looked around. The guards were taking the rest of the girls—six of them—to the end of the courtyard where the brick wall was. Now I saw a woman sweeping the cement floor in front of the wall as if cleaning the stage for actors to enter. I'd never seen a female janitor before. She had wrapped her black chador around her waist and was sweeping the courtyard with a small broom—too small for her task. The broom had a short handle and the woman had to hunch her back and bend low, close to the brick floor. The broom was shabby, too, very old, almost falling apart; it wouldn't do much. All of this indicated that the woman wasn't really cleaning the floor. She was an actor herself, pantomiming the act of sweeping. When the woman turned to me, I recognized Mrs. Moradi. I waved at her. She saw me, but hesitated for a moment and squinted her eyes to see me better. Then she recognized me, dropped the broom, and rushed toward me. Most of the girls in my line were inside the room now, sitting on the metal chairs. Only one girl was left in front of me. After her, it was my turn to enter. In the split second before Mrs. Moradi reached me, I thought that if she didn't get to me in time, I'd step into this room, and if I did, I'd never come out again. This was the last room of my life.

Mrs. Moradi approached me, gasping. "What are you doing here, child? I thought you were released!"

"No. They just wrote something on me and now I have to go into this room."

"Oh, no!" She covered her mouth with both hands. "I have to rush to Jamali and talk to him. It's a mistake. A horrible mistake." She unwrapped her chador from her waist, pulled it up on her head and ran to the building.

"Wait!" I called. "Why were you sweeping the yard?"

"I work here, dear. Now I'm a staff."

"No!"

"Yes, dear. When they killed Hamid they wanted to release me. I told them I didn't want to be in the free world anymore. I'll stay here and help Baba out. I'm a janitor now. I'm living where Hamid is," she said the last sentence while running toward the building.

"Where is he?" I screamed after her. I was confused.

"Behind The Wall of the Almighty. Buried behind that wall."

I looked at the wall. Now six guerrilla fighters were standing in front of it and a guard was blindfolding them.

"It's a horrible mistake," I heard Mrs. Moradi repeating to herself, panting and running.

34

One chair was left for me and it was next to a black curtain. Now Soghra emerged from behind the curtain and motioned with her forefinger. "Come!" I looked around to see if she was calling me. She was. I stepped behind the curtain. She showed me a narrow bed in a corner, a gray, woolen blanket covering it.

"Lie down," she said. Her voice was calmer than usual. This wasn't an order; it was more like a nurse talking to a patient.

I lay down and she told me to unbutton my uniform. My fingers were numb; she knew it too, because she didn't scold me for not being able to use my fingers. She did it for me. While she was squatting next to the bed, unbuttoning my uniform, I glanced at her watch. It was my watch. My father's digital watch. The green numbers flashed in the dim light of the chamber: 7:08. It was evening.

After Soghra unbuttoned all the buttons (there were many of them and they seemed to be increasing—an endless row of buttons), she called, "Come in! She's ready!"

I'm not sure from where, but from somewhere, maybe through the wall, a woman emerged. She was veiled from head to foot like Soghra herself. She came to the head of the bed and blindfolded me with a black scarf. It was right at this moment of absolute darkness when I heard one of the girls behind the curtain, in the waiting room, burst into sobs. She had just realized what was about to happen. Another girl hushed her, told her to be strong. Told her that our individual lives didn't matter and the revolution would succeed in the end and people would become free and hang these criminals with their turbans and chadors from the telephone poles. But this didn't stop the first girl from crying.

I'm not sure about the rest. My eyes were shut and I don't have an image I can call up. I just smelled the woman who was, for sure, the same woman I knew very well, but whose name I had never learned—the pock-marked woman. She had a peculiar smell of dust and dried dirt. Soghra called her Sister Sultani, and she said something to Soghra in her husky voice. In the darkness I imagined her dagger-shaped eyebrows penciled all the way to her temples. I imagined her burying corpses in the courtyard of the Bathhouse. That was where the smell of dirt came from. I heard the hollow sound of her shoes on the cement floor. Sister Sultani. So this was her name and she was whispering something above my head.

Now I heard someone else come in. A new odor: sweat and rust. Sister Sultani murmured something to this newcomer and then she recited a prayer. I could hear Soghra repeating the prayer a split second after her. I didn't hear the third person at all. Now one of them (Soghra?) held my arms from above and someone else removed my uniform. They pressed my arms down and I heard a scream—not my scream, one of the girls' in the room, because I'm sure that I remained mute and didn't utter a syllable when something pierced me and tore my insides. All I could imagine in that deep darkness I'd fallen into was Sister Sultani drilling a hole in me with her long forefinger.

35

A mountain of iron shattered, then collapsed. I opened my eyes and then closed them. In that brief second I realized that I was lying on a mat on the floor of a room, and not on the cement at the Wall of the Almighty. In that brief second I realized that I was alive. Knowing this, I closed my eyes. I wanted to sleep more. Drifting between sleep and wakefulness, I heard someone talking angrily above my head.

"I'm going to leave you here tonight, do you understand? You were a bad boy and I won't take you to the Holy Hills to watch the moon. You are being punished! Now stretch out your hands."

I heard the Whoop! Whoop! Whoop! of a rubber ruler, then a thin voice, the muffled voice of a trapped bird crying in his throat. The door banged and then there was silence. I listened to the silence. I was not drifting anymore. I opened my eyes and found myself face to face with the boy, Ali. Our positions were now reversed. I was lying on the floor, Ali sitting in the interrogation chair. We looked at each other for a long moment. I noticed Ali's long eyelashes framing his big black eyes. Now they were wet with tears and looked even longer. He sat there, his hands resting on his knees, palms up.

Jamali came in, Soghra following him. "Lift her up. I'm sick and tired of this shit. Mismanagement. Chaos. Irresponsibility. What was she doing out there, anyway?"

"Brother—" Soghra started, but couldn't go on. Jamali was mad.

"I don't want to hear any explanations. It's too late now. I'm supposed to be on the Holy Hills and I'm still here. Lift her up; let's take her out of here."

Soghra held my arms and lifted me up. We left the room.

"Sit right there and don't move, Ali," Jamali ordered his son. "If you cry, you'll get more whipping. I'll be back in a minute."

Soghra on my right, holding me up, almost dragging me, and Jamali on my left, we walked through the hall and reached the double wooden door. Jamali opened it with his key and we stepped out into the courtyard. The empty pool was filled with moonlight. It didn't look ugly anymore. It was clean, as if glowing with fresh, silvery water. At the Wall of the Almighty, Mrs. Moradi was washing off the blood with a hose. Her rubber-slippered feet were wet with blood and water. Bloody water splashed on her as she hosed the wall and the cement floor repeatedly.

"Watch this crazy woman for me," Jamali ordered Soghra. "She is acting as if she's watering a garden. I insisted that she go home, but she refused. She said she wanted to live here. But she is acting crazy now. Too much washing and sweeping. She gets on my nerves. If she talks to the inmates or does something stupid, send her to the Psychiatric Wing, where Robab and that loony girl—what's her name—are."

"Roya," Soghra said briefly.

"Yes. Send her where Robab and Roya are."

Now we reached the gate of the Bathhouse. On either side of the gate, two old lanterns sat on the wall, their lights flickering.

Jamali opened the gate and we stepped out. This was a street, with telephone poles and a few houses in the distance.

"Here take your stuff and go," Jamali shoved a bundle into my chest. "I don't know what to say, really. Don't you have a brain? Don't you have a tongue? No, I'm serious, couldn't you say something? Couldn't you tell that you were among the wrong people? Or maybe you wanted to be one of them, huh? Go now. This street ends at the main road. Can you see the taxis going toward town? Get a taxi and go home before the curfew."

"I want my watch back." I heard myself saying.

"What watch?" Jamali asked impatiently.

"My watch." I pointed to Soghra's hairy wrist.

"Is this her watch you're wearing, Sister?"

"I don't know. Someone must have given it to me. Here. What a big deal! You can buy this kind of watch by the kilo in the market," Soghra said and handed me the watch.

I wore the watch. The digits flashed 9:17.

Halfway down the street, I saw Baba pedaling on an old bicycle, coming toward the Bathhouse. He had a paper bag in one hand and held the handlebar with the other. When he saw me, he rang his bell and then stopped.

"Didn't I tell you, don't lose your spirit? Go now, it's hard to find a taxi. They're all heading toward the Holy Hills. Rush girl!"

I began to walk, but he stopped me again.

"Hey, wait! Do you want to see what I have in this paper bag? Guess!"

I looked at the bag, which was moving slightly in Baba's hand;

I couldn't make a guess. He waited a second and then slowly dipped his hand inside the bag and drew a pigeon out.

"I breed pigeons on the roof of my room. My male rock pigeon died, I bought this one. The poor woman needs a companion." He laughed, coughed, and spat thick phlegm out. Then he pedaled toward the prison. "Rush now, get yourself a taxi, girl!" He yelled.

When I reached the road, I stopped. Taxis, cars, and trucks were dashing by. For the first time, I realized that I was wearing my gray school uniform. Then I looked at the bundle in my arms. It was a man's shirt. Olive green color. Inside it there were three hardback journals. I threw the journals in the gutter of muddy water and wore the shirt over my school uniform. I walked farther up the road where there was more light and taxis were parked. A crowd of people rushed out of a gated garden, filling the cars and taxis. I heard the uproar of children, screams of joy, bursts of laughter. These were the sounds I had heard in the cell every night. I looked up because the sounds were coming from above. I saw roller coasters, carrousels, flying cars and space ships dashing and spinning, turning with dizzying speed. But suddenly they all stopped.

Now I felt a cramp in my belly, my knees buckled and I sat on a bench by the road. Warm blood gushed out from under me, spreading on the bench like a small lake. I sat in my blood, watching the children leaving the amusement park with their parents, heading toward home before the curfew. When the last family had left, and the last taxi had left, someone banged the park's heavy iron gate from inside, locked and bolted it. Now the last squeaks of the roller coasters and the rusty waltzes of the carrousels stopped. I sat on the bench until the city lights went off. The big yellow moon hung low above my head, and millions of stars twinkled in the dark. I felt cold, buttoned up the green shirt and lay down on the bench. I lay in my blood, looking at the sky, thinking. What would I tell my sister when she asked, What happened in the Bathhouse?